THE MYSTERY OF THE HAUNTED TRAIL

Janet Lorimer

AN
APPLE
PAPERBACK

SCHOLASTIC INC.
New York Toronto London Auckland Sydney

Acknowledgments

A heartfelt *mahalo* (thank you) to "Auntie" Betty Ann Rocha, a beautiful and knowledgeable lady who gave me a wealth of information and patiently checked my manuscript for accuracy. And to the wonderful staff of the Ewa Beach Public and School Library who helped me find research materials and gave me such encouragement.

ISBN 0-590-41830-0

12 11 10 9 8 7 6 5   1 2 3 4/9

Printed in the U.S.A.   ·   28

First Scholastic printing, February 1989

For David, husband and best friend,
who has always supported and encouraged me
in my endeavors, with love.

1

Brian pulled too hard on the screen door. It banged loudly against the wall. He winced, knowing what was coming next.

"Brian Kelly, don't bang that door!"

His mother's voice came from the laundry room. Brian tore into the house and raced toward the back. When he reached the laundry room, his mother glared at him over the top of her glasses.

"How many times — "

"Sorry, Mom, it was an accident. Did the letter come?"

" — have I told you — "

"Mom, please. This is important. Did it come?"

Mrs. Kelly sighed. "Yes, it came. It's upstairs on your bed. Now listen to me, Brian — "

"Thanks, Mom."

He wheeled around and dashed up the stairs, taking them two at a time.

The letter was on his pillow. He threw himself across the bed and grabbed it. His hands were beginning to shake. "Oh, please, let it be okay," he whispered before he opened it.

He ripped open the envelope and pulled out the letter, reading the first few lines. Then he leaped off the bed and grinned.

"I take it the news is good."

Brian turned and saw his mother leaning against the door frame. She was smiling and he knew she'd forgiven him.

"It's all set, Mom. Alani says he can hardly wait till I get there. Wow! It's really going to happen. I'm really going to Hawaii this summer."

Mrs. Kelly laughed. "I guess you are," she said. "That is exciting, Brian."

He sank back on the bed, his eyes shining. "I wish I could leave right now."

"The time will go by faster than you think," his mother said. "There's only a month of school left. You're going to need the time to get ready."

"I guess," Brian said, but he didn't sound convinced.

"Well, I'd better get back to work," Mrs. Kelly

said. "And speaking of work, don't forget your chores."

"Okay," Brian said, but he wasn't paying much attention. He was reading Alani's letter again.

"I want those garbage cans scrubbed before Dad gets home and the weeds by the fence pulled," his mother said.

"Yeah, right," Brian muttered.

There was a moment of silence. Then Mrs. Kelly added, "And you can wash my car, fix the roof, and paint the fence."

"Okay, Mom, I'll — " He looked up suddenly with a startled expression. "What?"

She laughed. "Just checking to see if you were paying attention. Don't forget those garbage cans, Brian, or else!"

He sighed. "Don't worry, Mom, I'll do it."

At last his mother left him alone. Brian read the letter for the third time. Alani was as excited about this trip as Brian was. The boys had been planning for over a year.

"We're going to have so much fun," Alani had written. "I'll teach you how to fish and body surf. We'll go to Kalawa so you can taste shave ice, too."

What in the world was shave ice? Brian wondered. As always, Alani wrote about some things that were totally foreign to Brian. But the boys did have other things in common. They both liked sports and hated social studies. They liked hamburgers and pizza, but neither one could stand liver or broccoli. They both had similar chores to do each day, like weeding the yard and taking out the trash. Neither of them liked to make his bed or write letters.

Writing letters! Brian grinned when he remembered that that's what had brought them together in the first place.

It had happened two years ago, when they were both in the fifth grade. Brian had been in class, staring out the window, watching the rain pour down on the playing field. Mrs. Roberts, his teacher, was giving out a social studies assignment, but Brian was barely listening.

"We've been studying about Hawaii for almost three weeks," Mrs. Roberts said. "I've decided it would be fun for you to write letters to a class of fifth-graders in Hawaii."

Most of the boys in the room groaned, including Brian. Mrs. Roberts' ideas about fun were definitely not theirs.

"This will be a good way for you to find out about Hawaii from the people who live there," the teacher went on. "You'll learn things that aren't in the textbook. So, when you write your letters, think about things you'd like to know. What do kids in Hawaii do to have fun? What kinds of food do they like to eat? What are their lives like?"

Brian slumped down in his chair and stared at the desk top. He hated this class! It was so boring! Who cared how people lived in Hawaii?

Brian wished it would stop raining so he could go outdoors. Track season would be coming up soon. Brian's feet itched to be practicing the fifty-yard dash and leaping hurdles. He sighed.

"You won't know who you're writing to," Mrs. Roberts went on. "But the students in Hawaii will write back. They'll answer your questions and probably ask you a few of their own. You can tell them what it's like to live here. Who knows? Maybe some of you will make new friends through these letters."

Big deal, Brian thought. He already had plenty of friends and he didn't have to write letters to them. This was such a dumb assignment. Besides, Mrs. Roberts would probably check his spelling and grammar and make him do it over until he got it just right.

His worst fears came true. "Brian, may I remind you that we are starting the third quarter of the school year?" Mrs. Roberts smiled as she handed him back his letter for the second time. "There is less than half a year left. Your social studies grade leaves a lot to be desired. But perhaps you won't mind missing track season this year in order to bring your grade up?"

Brian took the corrected letter from Mrs. Roberts and stalked back to his desk to do it over yet again.

At last the letter was written to Mrs. Roberts' satisfaction. And Brian soon forgot all about it. The track season started and he was busy practicing his hurdles. Maybe he would survive this school year after all.

It came as a surprise when Mrs. Roberts announced one day that a package of letters had arrived from Hawaii. Brian couldn't believe it when she handed one to him.

"I didn't write to anyone special," he said.

"Well, this particular boy has written to you, Brian. See? Your name is on the envelope."

Brian looked at the return address. The boy

was called Alani Nakoa. What a weird name! Brian wasn't sure how to say it. He opened the envelope, curious to see why this kid had sent him a letter.

Alani might have a strange name, but Brian and he seemed to have a lot in common. Brian thought it was funny that two kids could live in such different places and still like or dislike many of the same things. He began to wonder more about Alani. Did he have any hobbies? Any pets? Did he like track? Did they even have track in Hawaii?

There was only one way to find out. Brian wrote back. This time it was easy. He didn't have to have it checked by Mrs. Roberts.

He was pleased when Alani replied. He had to admit that getting letters was kind of fun. The boys exchanged photos, and for the first time, Brian got to see what his pen pal looked like.

Alani was mostly Hawaiian. He had been born and raised on Oahu. He lived on a farm in a place called Wailele Valley. In one of his letters, Alani explained that Wailele meant "waterfall." His mother, Mary Nakoa, was a nurse. She worked in a clinic in the small town of Kalawa. Alani's father, Joe, worked the farm with Alani's grandfather.

Alani called his grandfather Kupuna. The Hawaiian term for grandfather was *kupuna kane*.

Alani had an older brother, Keone, and a younger sister, Maile. And sure enough, he had a pet, a dog called Hupo. Brian laughed when Alani wrote that *hupo* meant "stupid."

In his picture, Alani wore a T-shirt and jeans. He was dark-skinned with black hair and dark eyes, and he had a big grin. He looked like he had a good sense of humor. Better still, he was wearing a baseball cap and a baseball mitt.

Brian had red hair and freckles. He had been born and raised in northern California and lived in a suburb of San Francisco. There were a lot of ways in which the boys were different, but in the things that counted, they were the same.

Brian and Alani kept writing. They finally got to meet during the summer after the sixth grade when Alani's family flew to southern California for a vacation. Mrs. Nakoa had cousins living in Pasadena. Brian's parents agreed to go to Pasadena, too, so the two boys could see each other in person. And from the moment they met, their friendship was sealed!

Brian liked Alani's parents, too. They insisted that he call them Auntie Mary and Uncle Joe.

"That's what children in Hawaii call most of their elders," Auntie Mary had said. "Even people they aren't related to." Brian had liked that custom. It made him feel like he belonged to the Nakoa family.

"You've just got to come to Hawaii," Alani said. "We could have so much fun."

"I know," Brian said, "but — " He stopped, gnawing his lower lip while he thought about it. He was an only child and sometimes his mother was so overly protective. Would she let him go all the way to Hawaii by himself?

When Alani heard how worried Brian was, he had said, "We'll just have to work on them," meaning their mothers. "We'll work on them till they say it's okay. Deal?"

"Deal!" Brian said.

And work they had! When his mother finally gave in and said yes, Brian could hardly believe it! So now it was all arranged. Alani's folks and Brian's folks had all agreed that the boys could spend a month together this summer. And summer was almost here!

"Brian!"

The sound of his mother's voice brought Brian

out of his daydream. Those darned garbage cans!
"Coming, Mom," he called.

As he went slowly downstairs, Brian remembered one sentence that puzzled him in Alani's letter. His friend had written: *There's been some strange stuff going on in the valley, but I'm not scared. And nothing's going to mess up our plans!*

Strange stuff? Scared? What was Alani talking about?

2

Brian could feel the plane begin to descend. The pilot was talking over the loudspeaker, telling the passengers that Diamond Head crater and the city of Honolulu could be seen from the right side.

The flight attendants hurried up and down the aisle, checking to make sure all the seat belts were fastened. Brian's hands turned clammy! Soon the plane would land, and he would actually be in Hawaii.

When Brian entered the busy terminal at Honolulu International Airport, he felt as if he'd stepped into another world! Everything seemed strange. People were hurrying in all directions, and Brian heard many strange languages — Japanese, Filipino, Samoan. He smelled the perfume from thousands of brightly colored garlands of flowers that he later learned were called *leis*. People carried them, wore them, and sold them in *lei* stands.

Hawaiian music was playing softly over the loudspeakers but every now and then, someone would make an announcement. The air was so warm and humid, Brian felt like he'd stepped into a steam room.

"Brian!"

He turned and saw Alani running toward him. Suddenly the scared feeling disappeared. Brian hollered and waved.

The whole family, with the exceptions of Kupuna and Hupo, the dog, had come to the airport. There were Alani's parents — "Uncle Joe" and "Auntie Mary," along with Alani's big brother, Keone, and his little sister, Maile. Maile greeted Brian with the *lei* she was holding. She motioned for Brian to bend down, and when he did, she slipped it over his head. At first he felt a little self-conscious to be wearing a necklace of flowers, but he was even more embarrassed when she kissed his cheek. "Aloha," she said softly. "Welcome to our Islands."

Brian straightened up quickly, feeling his

cheeks burn. Keone burst out laughing. "Hey, Brian, your face is as red as your shirt!"

Brian remembered that sixteen-year-old Keone loved to tease. He grinned at Keone, determined not to let the older boy's kidding get to him.

"My goodness, you've grown," Auntie Mary said. "Well, come on, everyone. Let's go find Brian's luggage and get out of here."

"Is it always this hot?" Brian asked as they hurried down to the baggage area.

"It always seems hotter here in town," Alani said. "When we get to the country, it will feel a lot cooler."

As they left the airport, Brian craned his neck, trying to see everything at once. "Honolulu's a big city," he said, surprised.

"It's our state capital," Auntie Mary answered. "Those mountains on your right are the Koolau Range. There is a notch in those mountains called Nuuanu Pali. In 1795 the great warrior chieftain Kamehameha I defeated the forces of Oahu in a terrible battle. Kamehameha and his warriors pushed the army of Oahu over the cliffs to their deaths, nearly 200 feet below. Of course, to be fair, some of the Oahuans preferred to leap off the cliffs, rather than be captured."

Keone groaned. "Not a history lesson, Mom. Not today! Brian just got here."

"Now you hush," Auntie Mary told her son. "This is all a part of our heritage. There are so many things for Brian to learn while he's here."

Brian didn't mind hearing stories like that one. It gave him goose bumps, just imagining the two armies battling on the high cliffs. There sure hadn't been anything like that in his history book!

Auntie Mary and Uncle Joe talked about Punchbowl, a great crater on the slopes above Honolulu. Punchbowl was also known as the National Memorial Cemetery of the Pacific. Many of the men buried there were from the famous 442nd Regimental Combat Team that fought during World War II.

"And did you know that the 442nd was made up of second-generation Japanese-Americans from Hawaii?" Auntie Mary asked. "That unit was highly decorated and, furthermore, they were all volunteers!"

They pointed toward Pearl Harbor, which the Japanese had attacked on December 7, 1941. "The battleship *Arizona* was blown up and sunk during the battle," Uncle Joe said. "There's a shrine built over the sunken ship. We'll take you out there before you go home."

Brian soon realized they were leaving the city behind. On each side of the freeway were fields and fields of green stalks, growing thickly together.

"Sugarcane," Alani said.

"After a while you'll see fields of pineapples," Auntie Mary added. "Pineapple and sugarcane are the state's two major crops."

Brian could not get over the colors! The green, green fields and the green mountains. The red earth, the blue sky, the yellow sunlight. Even the puffs of clouds that rode the horizon looked like huge white balls of cotton.

When they came over the top of a rise and started down the other side, Brian gasped. Ahead of him in the distance was the ocean. It was such a bright blue-turquoise. Brian thought it looked much more inviting here than it had in California. He couldn't wait to go swimming.

As they drove closer, Brian saw the roofs of buildings near the shore. "That's Kalawa," Auntie Mary said. "That's where I work."

"That's where we go to school," Maile piped up.

She smiled at Brian. He tried to smile back, but he had the funny feeling that Maile had a crush on him. That made him uncomfortable. After all, she was only ten.

"Not much farther now," Uncle Joe said as he slowed the station wagon on the narrow main street of the small town. Brian tried to see both sides of the street at once. He got an impression of old buildings sandwiched in with newer ones, small stores elbowing shops filled with tourist souvenirs. He saw side streets with small, neat houses and lush yards.

Huge trees shaded all the streets. Elderly men sat underneath on benches, and dogs lay at their feet, batting at flies with their tails.

When Kalawa was behind them, the highway narrowed even more. On one side of the road was the ocean, on the other, mountains.

Uncle Joe turned off onto a rutted track that led into the valley. Trees rose on each side of the road and the air was cooler. Brian could not hear the traffic sounds anymore, but in the distance, he still heard the boom of the surf.

Suddenly Keone grabbed his arm. "That's our place," he said, pointing. Brian saw a large, rambling house with a wide screened-in porch. There was paint flaking from the eaves and the roof was patched. But the yard was neat and tidy and there was a beautiful garden of flowers and grass.

And then he saw people coming from every direction. Lots and lots of people!

3

"Who are all those people?" Brian whispered to Alani.

"Our neighbors," Alani said. "They came to help with the *aha'aina*. That's what you would call a *luau*."

Luau was a word Brian remembered from Alani's letters. It meant a feast! And, in fact, Brian could smell food cooking. It seemed so long since he'd had lunch on the plane. His stomach rumbled.

"Our neighbors have farms here in the valley," Auntie Mary said. "We're like one big family, an *ohana*. Come, Brian. Everyone wants to meet you. They're all very excited about having you stay with us."

Brian began to feel shy at having to face so

many strangers. But he took a deep breath and followed Auntie Mary toward the crowd.

A tall, elderly man with white hair stepped forward to meet Brian first. His eyes and skin were the color of darkly polished wood.

"This is Kupuna," Auntie Mary said. "You may call him Kupuna, too, Brian."

Brian said, "Hello, sir," a little shyly and shook hands. Then, to his surprise, he felt himself swept up in a big bear hug.

"Goodness," Kupuna laughed. "Sir! That sounds too fancy. I'm just Kupuna. That's what all my grandchildren call me and now you are part of our family. Now, come and meet everyone else."

Brian heard so many strange names he knew he could never remember. He was given one *lei* after another until they were piled so high around his neck, they almost reached his nose. The sweet perfume of the flowers was overpowering.

Suddenly he was pushed hard from behind and almost fell over. He heard Keone roar with laughter, and when he turned to look, he saw a large yellow-and-brown dog about to lunge at him again. The dog didn't seem in the least bit angry.

19

His pink tongue lolled out of his mouth and he almost seemed to be laughing. Brian knew at once that this must be Hupo, and he reached out to pat the dog between his ears.

"Now you've met everyone," Alani said. "Come on, let's go in the house. I'll show you where we're going to sleep, and we can change out of these clothes."

The boys ran up the wooden steps to the screened-in porch. "This is the *lanai*," Alani said. "We're going to sleep out here. Usually I share a room with Keone, but Mom says that we can sleep here while you're visiting."

There were two cots at one end of the *lanai*. Scattered around the rest of the porch was a variety of mismatched furniture — chairs, an old sofa, and even a long bench covered with potted plants. "The plants belong to my mom," Alani said. "She even talks to them." He wrinkled his nose in disgust.

Brian laughed. "My mother grows roses," he said, "and she talks to them, too."

Brian opened one of his suitcases and pulled out a T-shirt and a pair of shorts. He kicked off his shoes and pulled off his socks and followed Alani.

The first room they passed was the kitchen, a

big room with cracked linoleum on the floor. Auntie Mary was standing at the stove, stirring something that bubbled in a big pot. Other women were clustered around the long tiled counter, slicing vegetables and talking.

"We're going to change," Alani told his mother, "and then I'll show Brian around."

"Don't go too far," Auntie Mary said. "We'll be eating soon. And don't get in the way."

The boys passed through the large living room that Alani called the parlor. The floor was covered with rattan mats and the furniture was wood with brightly colored cushions. A narrow hall led from the parlor to the bedrooms and bathroom. It was such a cozy, comfortable house, Brian knew he'd feel at home here.

After the boys had changed to cooler clothes and Brian had removed the heavy layer of flower *leis*, the boys tore outdoors.

Long tables had been set up in the yard, and women and children were busily laying out dishes and silverware. Smoke was coming from a deep pit on the other side of the yard. Alani explained that the pit was an *imu*, an underground oven. Kupuna and Uncle Joe had dug it the day before. They had filled the *imu* with wood and lighted a fire. Then they had heated rocks in the fire before adding a layer of wet banana and *ti* leaves. Uncle Joe had put food on the leaves, and Kupuna had covered the food with more leaves and a layer of canvas and gunny sacks. The whole thing had then been covered with earth. Heat and steam had cooked the food overnight. Now the men were opening the *imu* to take out the cooked food.

It smelled heavenly and Brian's stomach rumbled again. Auntie Mary called to everyone to gather around the tables. Kupuna said a blessing and the feast began.

Platters and bowls of food were passed so quickly that Brian gave up trying to figure out what everything was. He recognized chicken and potato salad and barbecued ribs. But some of the other dishes were very strange. Alani tried to help him out. "That's *lomi* salmon. It's really good. That's pickled *limu*. Try some."

"What's *limu?*" Brian asked suspiciously.

Keone grinned. "Seaweed." He burst out laughing at the expression on Brian's face.

"Try it," Alani urged. "It's good."

Brian put some in his mouth. He had to admit it wasn't all that bad, although it did taste a little fishy.

But he drew the line at *poi*. The grayish paste was awful. Keone laughed again at Brian's reaction. "What's the matter, Brian. Don't you like it?"

"Don't pay any attention to Keone," Auntie Mary said. "There are lots of things he doesn't like to eat, either."

Although Brian was determined to taste everything, he was soon full. So was Alani. The boys excused themselves.

The sun was going down. Mosquito coils were lighted and their smoke drove the insects away. Small children darted around the yard, playing games and laughing. The grown-ups began to clear the tables.

The air was filled with the strange odors of the food, the pungent odor of the mosquito coils, and the sweet fragrance of flowers. It was all so strange, Brian thought, and yet wonderful, too. He almost believed he had stepped into another world.

His long day was beginning to catch up with him. He felt very sleepy. Then, abruptly, he heard angry voices at the end of the table.

"I tell you, it makes no sense. There's been no drought this year. We should have plenty of water. Remember the rains we had this spring? Water should be the least of our problems. But no, the stream dries up more each day. Something is going on, something that scares me!"

Brian looked at the group of men gathered at the end of the table. The happy, easygoing group was suddenly tense.

"Well, I've had it. I've lost most of my tomato plants and the onions, too. They were doing just fine. Now, they're all dead. Tell me how that could happen overnight?"

"It's the night marchers. I've heard them on the old haunted trail. They're angry with us."

Everyone fell silent. Brian craned his neck, trying to see who was speaking. It was a small man in a red shirt. The festive mood of the *luau* vanished.

"There are too many strange things going on," the small man said. "Never, in all the years I've lived in this valley, have I seen such bad times."

Several of the other men nodded. "It's not like it was in the old days," one of them said. "I never worried about my crops before. But now — "

"I've lost half my crops," another man said. "And for no reason! One day the plants are healthy, the next day they are dead! And the water is drying up for no reason."

The man in the red shirt rose to his feet and shook his fist in the air. "This valley has been cursed," he exclaimed. "The gods must be angry with us. They no longer smile on our way of life. They take away the water and they kill our plants. How much longer can we stay here?"

"That's enough, Alfredo!" Kupuna rose to his feet, too. He towered, like an angry giant, over the smaller man. "Alfredo, you and I have been friends for years. We were born in this valley, we grew up here. We listened to the stories our elders told us, stories about the gods and the ancient Hawaiians and how they first came to settle in this valley. You know as well as I do that this talk of curses is nonsense."

"Then explain why our water dries up to a trickle. Explain why the crops die," the smaller man hissed angrily. He glared at Kupuna and Brian saw Kupuna wince.

"Who's that man?" Brian whispered to Alani.

"Alfredo Fernandez," Alani whispered back. Brian saw that Alani was frowning. "He and grandfather have been friends for years. But now — "

"What are they talking about?" Brian asked. "What's all this about a curse?"

Alani looked very uncomfortable. "I-I don't know," he said and Brian knew, somehow, that Alani was not telling the truth. It surprised him because they had always been able to talk about everything.

Then Brian remembered the line from Alani's letter, the mysterious line about strange things going on in the valley. And suddenly Brian had the feeling that Alani was scared.

"I can't explain why these things are happening, Alfredo," Kupuna said more quietly. "But — "

"Ah, you see?" Mr. Fernandez turned to the others with a smile. "Even he has no explanation. I don't know about the rest of you, but I'm thinking of leaving the valley."

Some of the men looked shocked, but others nodded in agreement. Kupuna stiffened. "That's not the answer," he growled. "Our lives are here. But not just our lives, the lives of our children and our grandchildren are here, too. We must be patient and strong. There is an answer for the things that have happened to us. Running away will solve nothing."

"That's easy for you to say," one of the other men called out. "You haven't lost any crops."

Kupuna turned on the man, but before he could speak, Auntie Mary stood up and said in a loud, clear voice, "Kupuna, Uncle Alfredo. Have you forgotten that this is a party? And we have a guest?"

Everyone turned to look at Brian. Kupuna's angry frown disappeared. "Of course," he said. "This is not the time nor the place to talk about these things."

The others nodded and tried to smile. Someone began to strum a ukulele and several people sang along. But Brian could still feel the tension.

Two phrases the men had used earlier kept running around in his head. The night marchers! The old haunted trail! Where was this trail, Brian wondered, and who or what were the night marchers?

Something was wrong in this beautiful valley. Something was terribly wrong!

4

Jet lag had begun to catch up with Brian. His body told him that it was three hours later than what the clock said. As the last guests said good-night and departed, Brian was having trouble keeping his eyes open.

When Brian and Alani went to say good-night to Kupuna, they found him sitting on the front steps, scratching Hupo between his ears. Kupuna smiled when the boys sat down beside him.

"Tired?" Kupuna asked.

Brian nodded, stifling a huge yawn.

"It was fun," Alani said, his eyes shining. "And the food was great! I'm stuffed." He rubbed his stomach with satisfaction.

Kupuna laughed. "I was watching you, Alani. You ate enough food for three boys. How are you doing, Brian? Does it all seem very strange?"

"Sort of, " Brian said. "But it's a nice kind of strange."

Kupuna smiled. "It's good that you can open up your mind and heart to something new, Brian. A lot of people can't do that. Now you boys better get to bed."

Alani stood up but Brian hesitated. "Kupuna," he said, "what are the night marchers?"

There was a long silence. Alani wiggled uncomfortably. "Come on, Brian," he said, "Kupuna's right. Time we got to bed."

"Wait, Alani," Kupuna said. "Sooner or later, Brian, you will hear more about the night marchers. I'd just as soon tell you about them myself so that you hear the truth."

Alani sat down again and the two boys looked at Kupuna.

"The night marchers," said Kupuna, "are ghosts, the spirits of our ancestors who walk the old trails."

Ghosts! Brian shuddered.

"We call them the *Huaka'i po*, the Marchers of the Night," Kupuna went on. "Sometimes the ghostly procession is made up of the gods, sometimes it is a procession of warriors, and sometimes it is a procession of ordinary people. They walk the old trails on certain nights that are dedicated to four of our gods — Ku, Lono, Kane, and Kanaloa. There are a number of these nights each month.

"The Kane nights are the darkest nights of all. In olden times they were so sacred, no noise was allowed. Everyone stayed indoors. If you were caught making noise or if you went outside, you could end up as a sacrifice."

Brian shuddered again. When he'd studied Hawaii in the fifth grade, Mrs. Roberts had never said a word about ghosts and sacrifices.

"Sometimes," Kupuna went on, "the spirits march in single file, sometimes in ranks. If someone should stumble across the night marchers, that person risks death at the hands of a ghostly spearsman. Of course, if the person is a relative of one of the dead marchers, he will undoubtedly be allowed to live."

"How can you tell when the night marchers are coming?" Brian asked.

"First you hear the sound of drums and perhaps the nose flute. Then you may hear the sound of chanting."

"What do you do if you see them?"

"You have several choices," Kupuna said. "The

first and best choice is to run away and hide. You don't look back and you make as little noise as possible. You want to leave without attracting their attention."

"That's what I'd do," Alani said. "I'd run like crazy."

"If there is no time to run and hide, then you must assume the *kapu moe* position to avoid having the spear thrown at you," Kupuna said. "You take off all your clothes and lie down with your eyes closed."

"But the spear isn't real," Brian asked. "Is it?"

"Let me tell you a story about that," Kupuna said. "This happened when I was a small child. I was visiting my cousins who lived near the beach. One night as we were getting ready for bed, we heard drums and chanting.

"My auntie knew it was the night marchers, walking the old trail that led down to the shore. She was terrified. She made us children hide under the covers and remain quiet. She said we were to pretend to be asleep. And she did the same thing! We were all so frightened that our hearts seemed to beat as loudly as those ghostly drums. But we did exactly as we were told. We did not move. We heard the drums coming closer

31

and closer. Then they passed us and we heard the sounds disappear."

He was silent for a moment and Brian swallowed hard.

"The next day," Kupuna went on, "we learned that the neighbors had found the body of an old Japanese fisherman on the rocks at the base of the cliff. He had been there the night before, night fishing. He was very deaf, you see, and he had not heard the night marchers. There was no relative in the procession to stop the spearsman. They said he died of a heart attack but . . . " Kupuna's voice trailed away.

"But what?" Brian urged. Despite the warm air, he felt cold all over.

"That man had a heart as sound as a bell," Kupuna said softly.

Brian didn't know what to think. Had the fisherman really died of a heart attack? Or had he been the victim of a ghostly spearsman?

"Kupuna," Alani said, "why does Uncle Alfredo say the night marchers are angry with us?"

Kupuna made a sound of disgust. "Alfredo is a fool. The night marchers don't destroy plants or dry up streams. They are not the cause of our troubles."

"But people say they've heard the drums and chanting," Alani said.

Kupuna frowned. He was silent for a long moment. Then he put a large hand on each boy's shoulder. "Listen to me," he said. "I can't explain why these things are happening in our valley, but I know it is not because of the *Huaka'i po*. Something else is going on. I know there is an explanation."

Brian was fascinated by the story. A little scared, he had to admit, but very curious.

"Alani," he said, "will you show me the haunted trail? Maybe tomorrow we could — "

"No!" Alani almost shouted. Brian looked at him in surprise.

"No, Brian," Kupuna said more gently. "That old trail leads far into the valley. And that is no place for a boy who is a stranger. It's not that I would worry about you being on the trail. You see, there are other dangers, very real dangers in the valley. The trees and brush grow very thick. The mountains are steep and treacherous. People with a lot of experience have gotten lost or been hurt trying to climb our mountains. I have made all my grandchildren promise never to go into the far end of the valley without an adult along. And that means you must promise, too. If anything happened to you, I would never forgive myself."

"Okay," Brian promised. He was sobered by these warnings, but a part of him still wanted to see that haunted trail.

"And now," Kupuna said, "it is really time for bed. Look at Hupo. He knows."

The boys looked at the dog and laughed. Hupo was curled up into a little brown-and-yellow ball, his tail under his nose. Now and then his ears twitched as if he were having some happy doggy dream.

"Kupuna," Alani said, "that dumb dog sleeps most of the time anyway. Unless he's chasing a mongoose!"

Kupuna chuckled. "That's true," he agreed. "Well, you two can stay up all night for all I care. But don't blame me when the alarm clock goes off and you want to hide your heads under the covers instead of having fun."

He stood up and stretched. The boys could take a hint. They stood up, too, and said good-night.

Later, after they crawled into their beds, they talked in low voices. "Tomorrow I'll show you around," Alani said. "There's a lot to see."

"Can we go to the ocean?" Brian asked. "I want to learn how to body surf."

"Not tomorrow," Alani said. "First, Kupuna says we have to see how well you swim. I'll take you to the stream. There's a pool we swim in, and maybe we can even catch some fish."

That sounded good to Brian. He didn't care what he swam in, as long as it was wet.

Before he fell asleep, Brian was wondering if tonight he'd hear the sound of drums and ghostly chanting and . . .

Suddenly a shaft of morning light awakened him. He blinked and sat up. Was it daylight already? Then he heard the sounds of the family stirring and he smelled breakfast smells. His stomach rumbled. He leaned over and tugged Alani's pillow. "Wake up," he laughed.

The boys dressed quickly and went to breakfast. Auntie Mary was hurrying to get ready for work. She looked so different in her nurse's uniform. Uncle Joe and Kupuna were just finishing their meal. Keone and Maile were still eating, too, and Keone was trying to steal a piece of bacon from his sister's plate.

"And what are your plans for the day?" Auntie Mary asked Alani.

"I'm going to show Brian around," he explained.

"Well, don't forget your chores," Auntie Mary said.

"But, Mom, Brian is company. He doesn't have to do chores," Alani said.

"Brian, are you company or are you family?" Auntie Mary smiled.

"Family," Brian grinned, knowing what was coming next.

"Good!" Auntie Mary laughed. "And family members all do chores! See you tonight!"

After the boys had finished their chores, they took off. There was so much to see. Alani explained that the valley was quite large. "A long time ago, about a thousand Hawaiians lived here," he said. "Now, there are only about a dozen families in the valley."

"Are they all Hawaiian?" Brian asked.

"No, not all. There are some Japanese families, some Filipino families, Portuguese, Samoan, Chinese. . . ." He ticked off the nationalities on his fingers. "And lots of mixtures, too. My great-grandmother was Chinese and I'm part Portuguese, too."

"That's like my family," Brian said. "I'm mostly

Irish on my dad's side, but also English and Scottish. And German on my mom's side."

Alani grinned. "Hey, you know what? Between us, we represent most of the world!"

Brian laughed. "We're like the United Nations, rolled into two kids."

Alani led Brian down the dusty road, past one farm after another. There were fields filled with taro, lettuce, tomatoes, onions, ginger, and daikon, a kind of white radish.

Alani pointed out bananas, papayas, and mangoes growing on strange-looking trees. Brian had never seen papayas or mangoes before. But he did recognize the avocado trees.

Soon the dusty road narrowed into a trail. "We'll go see the stream," Alani said. "It will feel good to swim after all this walking."

But when they reached the stream, Alani stopped and stared at it, frowning. Even Brian could see that something was wrong. The water level was at least a foot below the banks.

"I don't understand it," Alani said. "It's dropped even more."

"Maybe something has blocked the streams higher up," Brian said.

Alani shook his head. "Uncle Alfredo went into

the valley to see if the stream needed to be cleaned out. But he said it was running fine. How can water just disappear like this?"

"Let's go see that pool you talked about," Brian said, wanting to cheer his friend up.

"Okay," Alani said. "We follow the stream up a little way."

Before long they came to the pool. "I wish we could go swimming," Brian said wistfully. The cool water looked so inviting.

Alani laughed. "Well, of course we can," he said. "What's to stop us?"

"We didn't bring our trunks," Brian said.

"Who needs trunks?" Alani laughed, leaping into the water feet first. Brian didn't need an invitation.

When they were tired of splashing each other, the boys crawled out onto the grassy bank and lay in the sun. Before long, they were completely dry, clothes and all.

Alani couldn't wait to show Brian the strawberry guava tree that grew nearby. The boys picked the fruit and ate it. The tiny red balls were filled with seeds but delicious. And Alani and Brian had a wonderful time spitting the seeds at each other!

It was mid-afternoon when the boys started for home. When they reached the spot where the trail widened into the road, Brian noticed that the trail also forked, branching off in a different direction. He couldn't see where it went because it was so overgrown, but he thought it led toward the mountains.

"Where does that trail go?" he asked.

Alani stiffened. "Into the valley," he said and began to walk faster.

"Hey, wait a minute." Brian scrambled to keep up. "Can we take that trail tomorrow?"

Alani shook his head. "It isn't used much," he said. "It's all overgrown and it isn't safe."

"Why not?"

Alani stopped walking and turned to look at Brian. "We have to stay away from that trail. Kupuna would be really mad if we ever hiked on it."

"Why?" Brian said.

"Because," Alani said, "that's the old trail. The haunted trail!"

5

Everyone rose early the next day, even before the sun was up. Auntie Mary had to get ready for work; the men had to get ready to tend their fields. And the children had, as always, morning chores.

Not only were crops grown in the valley, but animals were also raised — chickens, pigs, cows, and goats. The Nakoas had chickens. It was up to Brian and Alani to collect the eggs, feed the chickens, and clean out the chicken coop. Brian didn't mind collecting their eggs, but cleaning up after them was something else.

"Just be glad we don't have pigs or goats," Alani said. "Uncle Alfredo keeps pigs. Phew!" He wrinkled his nose in disgust.

"Why does he keep pigs?" Brian asked.

Alani laughed. "What do think you ate at the *aha'aina* the other night? Where do you think that pig came from? We trade with each other — milk, eggs, meat."

"Wow! You raise almost everything you eat," Brian said.

Alani nodded. "But it's hard work, too. Still, I really like it."

Brian agreed it was hard, but he was beginning to like it, too.

Just before Kupuna and Uncle Joe left to tend their crops, Keone cornered his father. He wanted to take Brian and Alani to Kalawa for the day. "We can show Brian around," Keone said, "and take him to the beach."

Uncle Joe looked thoughtful. Then he smiled at Brian. "How about it, Brian? Would you like to go?"

"Oh, yes, sir!" Brian said.

"What about me?" They all turned to look at Maile. Alani groaned a little and Brian knew that the other boys didn't want to be saddled with a little sister.

Uncle Joe looked at his sons with a stern look. "Keone, you know the rule. If one goes, all go!"

"Yes, sir," Keone said. Brian saw that Keone had crossed his fingers behind his back. He knew that Keone wanted to go very badly.

"And you boys will have to take care of your sister. Understand?" He looked at all three of them. They all nodded.

"Does that mean we can go?" Keone asked.

"Yes, I guess you can," Uncle Joe said. He fished a set of keys from his pocket. "Now remember, Keone, you drive carefully."

"Yes, sir!"

"No silliness and no showing off. You drive slowly the whole time."

"Yes, sir."

Alani leaned over and whispered in Brian's ear, "Keone just got his driver's license."

Brian looked at Keone with new respect. He could hardly wait for the day when he could get his license, but his parents had already told him it was light years away.

"You'd better pack a big lunch," Uncle Joe added. "I know how you boys eat, so take enough for everyone. Oh, and one more thing. You stay at the beach at Kalawa. I don't want you going somewhere else where the waves are bigger."

"Sir?" Keone said, a puzzled look on his face.

"You know what I mean," Uncle Joe said. "No surfing!"

Keone looked heartbroken. "No surfing?"

"You kids can take boogie boards and do a little body surfing. But that's it! I know the waves at Kalawa are very small in the summer and I like it like that! We have to think about Brian's safety, too, you know."

"I can swim," Brian said helpfully to Uncle Joe.

"I'm sure you can," Uncle Joe smiled, "but I'd feel better if you were all at Kalawa, where the water is calmer."

The kids worked quickly to pack a lunch and collect their gear. They stowed everything into the back of Uncle Joe's truck. Brian and Alani rode in back while Maile rode up front with Keone.

When they reached Kalawa, Keone found a place to park in the shade.

"Let's show Brian the town first," Alani said. The others agreed and they all wandered up and down the main street, peering into shop windows and making jokes about the tourists. Keone told Brian that Kalawa was a favorite tourist spot in the summer because of its quaint buildings and beautiful beach.

"How about a swim?" Alani called out as he crossed the road and headed to the beach.

The moment his feet hit the smooth sand, Brian felt like he was in heaven. Before him stretched a wide, white sandy beach, dotted with coconut palms.

They found a shady spot under a coconut palm and laid out their straw beach mats. The boys stripped down to their swim trunks and Maile to her bathing suit. Then they raced into the water.

Brian was surprised to find it so warm. Alani challenged him to a race while Keone stayed behind to watch Maile. Alani won, but not by much.

After Brian and Alani had done some swimming, they climbed onto the warm sand. It was their turn to stay with Maile, while Keone swam.

Alani told Brian that the waves could get very high in the winter. "That's when we have surfing contests," Alani said. "When the waves are thirty feet high, look out!"

Brian had to stifle a grin at Alani's use of the word "winter." He couldn't imagine having a beach picnic or swimming in December, but he knew that here in Hawaii the weather was very mild most of the year.

Maile wanted to hunt for shells, and she begged Brian to walk down the beach with her. At first Brian didn't really want to, but finally he gave in. There were many beautiful shells drying in the sun. Maile found a spotted tiger cowrie. "It's supposed to be good luck," she told Brian. "Here, you take it!" And she pushed the sun-warmed shell into his hand.

"I'm starving," Keone exclaimed when he came out of the water. They decided to eat their picnic lunch under the palm tree. The delicious lunch of sandwiches and lemonade made everyone a little drowsy. After they ate, they all stretched out on the mats and half dozed in the heat.

Finally Keone sat up. "Let's get the boards and hit the water before we have to leave," he said. "Brian, want to learn to ride a boogie board?"

The boogie boards were made of styrofoam and shaped like small surfboards. Brian soon mastered the art of paddling out toward the reef, turning the board, and riding one of the low waves back to shore. It was really easy, he decided, and he was beginning to feel a little cocky.

Suddenly, he heard Keone shout. He just had time to glance over his shoulder and see a very large wave speeding toward him. Then, caught by the wave, he was thrown off his board. Over and over he tumbled underwater.

When the wave deposited him roughly on the shore, he sat up, coughing and wiping the salt water out of his eyes.

As soon as Keone reached him and saw he was all right, the older boy couldn't resist teasing him. "You gotta be careful, Brian. Those big waves can sneak up on you. Man, that one was a real killer. All of two, no, three feet! Now, that's a wave!"

Brian felt himself turning red and it wasn't from the sun. "Knock it off, Keone," Maile yelled. "It's not funny."

"It's okay, Maile," said Brian. He really wished she'd stop taking his side, but he didn't want to hurt her feelings, either.

Alani saved them all from further embarrassment. "Hey, Keone, look at the sun. It's getting late."

Keone agreed it was time to go. They collected their gear and headed back for the truck.

After they had stowed their things in the truck, Maile said, "We've got to get a shave ice, Keone. Please!"

Keone nodded. Brian remembered that Alani

had mentioned shave ice in one of his letters. He hoped it was something he would like.

"Don't worry," Alani said, when he saw the doubtful look on Brian's face. "You'll love shave ice. It's like a snow cone."

Brian grinned. Snow cones were one of his favorite treats, especially on a hot day. The four hurried to a small grocery store on the corner.

It was an old building, and inside Brian saw shelves of everything from dusty-topped cans to cellophane-wrapped bread. There were jars filled with strange-looking foods that Alani explained were kimchee and crack seed.

When Brian saw a rack of postcards, he remembered he should send a note to his parents. He looked at T-shirts, rubber thongs, beach mats, suntan lotion, fish hooks, bamboo poles to make into fishing rods, fishnets, children's toys, magazines in several languages, a stack of newspapers, and —

"Hey, Brian, what flavor do you want?" Keone called.

Brian chose lime and watched as a machine shaved the ice that was scooped into paper cones, then topped with a green syrup. Maile's was cherry red and Alani chose blue vanilla. But

Keone went all out with a rainbow cone that had every color and flavor of syrup on the shelf.

While Brian waited for the others, he took another walk around the store. He saw posters advertising soft drinks and dog food from years before. And high up in the dark corners, he saw masses of cobwebs. The windows were so grimy, hardly any light came into the large room.

The kids took their snow cones outside and sat on a bench. Brian noticed that the bench was old and scarred.

"What is this place?" he muttered to Alani.

"Shimoda's," Alani said. "It's been here for years. They don't sell a lot of groceries anymore because most people shop at the new shopping center. But they have the best shave ice in the world!"

Brian agreed with that. He sucked the sweet, cold cone slowly. It was the perfect snack after a day at the beach.

Just as the four were about to climb into the truck, Maile shouted, "Hey, look, there's Uncle Alfredo." She jumped up and down and waved. "Hi, Uncle Alfredo," she called.

The boys turned to look and saw Alfredo Fernandez standing across the street. He was talking to two men. One was dressed in a business suit and Brian thought it looked out of place in this small, old-fashioned town. The other man was dressed more casually but he was huge — built like a wrestler.

Alfredo turned at the sound of his name. But when he saw the four chidren, he got a strange look on his face. He didn't smile or call out a greeting. Instead, he quickly turned his back.

Maile looked hurt. "What's wrong with him?" she asked Keone. "He acts like he doesn't know us."

"Oh, he's probably just busy," Keone said, helping her into the truck.

Brian and Alani climbed into the back. "Who are those men?" Brian asked.

"The guy in the suit is Mr. Lee," Alani said. "He's a businessman. No one likes him very much. He's always trying to buy land and build more buildings. You know, offices, hotels, and stuff like that."

"Who's the other guy, the big one?"

"Everyone calls him Tako," Alani said. Then seeing the look on Brian's face, he laughed. "Not taco," he exclaimed. And he spelled out the name. "T-A-K-O. It means 'squid.' He works for Mr. Lee. No one likes him, either."

"Why is Mr. Fernandez talking to them?"

Alani shrugged. "Beats me. Mr. Lee is always trying to get the farmers in the valley to sell their land to him. Maybe he knows Uncle Alfredo is thinking of leaving the valley, and he wants to make an offer for his farm. Uncle Alfredo sure doesn't look very happy."

Unhappy didn't quite describe it, Brian thought. Alfredo Fernandez had looked more than unhappy. He had looked downright afraid!

6

Kupuna chuckled when Brian told him that evening about the wave that had attacked him.

"Never underestimate the power of the ocean, Brian. You should always respect it."

"Tell Brian the story about the chief who loved to surf and was turned to stone," Alani said.

Kupuna smiled. "A story, eh? Very well. Once, long ago . . ."

Kupuna spoke softly, and in his mind Brian could see the tale unfold as Kupuna told it. It was the story of a handsome Hawaiian chief who came to the North Shore to surf. One day a beautiful girl saw the young man and sent her pet sea-birds to bring him to her. The birds did as they were told and the young couple met. They fell in love and were married. And their lives were very happy.

Now the young chief loved to surf. Every time he left his pretty wife to go surfing, she would make two garlands of *lehua* blossoms for him to wear. But one day, when he reached the shore, another girl greeted him with a *lei* of *ilima* blossoms.

The sea-birds saw this and flew to tell the chief's wife. When her husband returned, she saw that he was wearing an extra *lei*. She was very angry. She called upon her ancestral gods to punish him. The chief felt his body become very heavy. He turned to have one last look at his beloved beach as his body turned to stone.

"And to this day, the stone still stands. One of these days we'll take you to see it," Kupuna said.

Brian and Alani begged for another story and then another. Kupuna told them the stories his grandfather had told him. There was the story of Pele, the goddess of the volcano, and Maui, the god who tried to join all the islands with his great hook. There were stories of the *menehune*, the race of small people who were renowned builders, and stories of the shark gods.

Finally Kupuna said, "And now it's time for bed."

Brian and Alani groaned at the same time. "Oh, please, Kupuna, just one more."

Kupuna chuckled. "Just one more will wear out my throat. Besides, what will we do tomorrow night if I tell you all my stories now?"

The boys laughed and agreed that it would be better to wait.

After he climbed into bed, Brian thought about the strange and wonderful stories Kupuna had told him. There were all sorts of pictures swimming in his head. Pictures of another time, another world, another people so unlike anything he had ever known.

Outside crickets sang and a gecko, a little lizard, chirruped as it hunted for insects. Brian could hardly keep his eyes open. He could hear Alani breathing evenly. His friend was already asleep.

The next thing Brian knew he was somewhere else! He looked around, bewildered, trying to discover where he was. All around him was thick, lush growth. Trees, bushes, ferns, and tangled vines made green walls. Then he saw that he was standing on a trail that wound through the jun-glelike growth. But not just any trail! Somehow he knew he was deep inside the valley on the forbidden haunted trail.

Brian knew he had to get off the trail. He had to get home. But every time he tried to take a step, the vines reached out to stop him. They wound themselves around his arms and legs. He struggled to break free.

Suddenly, beneath the sound of his ragged breathing, he heard something. Brian froze, lis-tening. In the silence, he heard the sound of chanting; the words were strange to him. Strange and frightening. Could it be the night marchers?

Brian was terrified! He struggled harder than ever and, as if by magic, the vines fell away. He tried to run but his legs would not obey. They were so heavy, and when he looked down, he saw that they had turned to stone! He cried out in terror and . . .

His eyes snapped open!

He was sitting up in bed, bathed in sweat, breathing in short gasps.

For a moment, he could not move. His whole body felt weak and shaky. A dream! It had only been a silly dream! He swallowed hard but his mouth was still dry. Silly, maybe, but scary and very real.

Little by little Brian began to relax. He turned to see if Alani had woken up, but his friend was still sound asleep. What a relief! Brian would have died of embarrassment if his nightmare had awakened Alani. Alani would have thought it was funny. And if Keone knew, Brian knew he would tease him.

He edged down under the covers. It was all because of those stories and legends Kupuna had told. Brian forced himself to think about the fun he'd had at the beach. And in the town, window shopping. And the shave ice! He concentrated on the taste of the sweet syrup and the way the ice had felt on the tip of his tongue.

At first the drumming was so low that Brian almost didn't hear it. The crickets were making a lot of noise. But as the drumming grew louder the insects grew silent, as if fearful of the new sounds.

Brian raised his head a little way off the pillow. And that was when he heard the voices softly chanting with the drums!

Brian was terrified. It was a dream! It had to be! It couldn't be real.

But at the same time, he knew he was not asleep. He was lying in his bed in the Nakoa house and he was wide awake. In the distance he heard the same terrifying sounds he had dreamed about just a few minutes ago.

It couldn't be real! It had to be his imagination!

But as the sounds grew louder and closer, he knew he was not imagining it. What he was hearing was real! It was the *Huaka'i po*, the Marchers of the Night!

Brian's heart began to pound; his mouth went dry again. What should he do? Should he wake Alani and tell him? Or should he wake one of the adults? He was too scared to do anything.

Brian dived under the covers, pulling them tightly over his head. He squeezed his eyes shut and wished he could shut his ears, too. He lay as still as possible.

With the covers over his head, the drumming and chanting were muffled and bit by bit seemed to grow fainter. Brian began to relax. In the cocoon of his blanket, he felt safe.

The next thing he knew, he was being shaken. "Come on, Brian, wake up! Are you going to sleep all day?" It was the familiar voice of Alani, and never before had anything sounded so good.

Brian threw back the covers and stared sleepily at his friend. He yawned and blinked. "What time is it?"

"Time to get up," Alani said. "Boy, when you sleep, nothing wakes you up!"

By the time Brian got to the table, the rest of the family had almost finished eating. Auntie Mary smiled at him. "Well, sleepyhead, I guess all that sun and surf got to you!"

"We thought you'd never wake up," Uncle Joe laughed. "You must have slept like a log."

"No!" Brian said. "I didn't. Not really. See, I had this awful dream about hearing the night marchers. But then I woke up and it was true! It was —"

He realized they were all staring at him as if he'd just lost his mind. He wished he'd kept quiet, but now that he'd started, he couldn't stop. He told them the whole story.

Keone burst out laughing. He rocked back and forth on his chair until he nearly fell off.

"Keone, stop that," Auntie Mary said sharply. But then Brian saw that her lips were twitching as if she were trying hard to keep from smiling. Uncle Joe was biting his lower lip and Kupuna had a hand over his mouth. Alani was grinning from ear to ear.

"It's true," Brian said. "It really happened. You have to believe me!"

"Oh, that's great," Keone gasped, wiping his eyes. "That's classic, Brian. Boy, I'd love to see what you do after you see a horror movie. Do the werewolves come and tickle your toes?"

"Shut up, Keone," Maile yelled. "Just shut up!"

"Maile, don't tell your brother to shut up. Keone, stop teasing!" Auntie Mary said crossly. Then, in a more kindly voice, she said to Brian, "Everyone has bad dreams now and then. And they can seem very real, Brian. But that's all it was. Just a bad dream."

Brian felt such a sense of despair. Why wouldn't they believe him? "It wasn't a dream," he said. "Honest, Auntie Mary — "

The shrill jangle of the telephone interrupted him.

"I'll get that," Auntie Mary said. When she left the table, Uncle Joe turned to Alani. "Well, son, what are you boys going to do today?"

Before Alani could answer, Kupuna said, "I'd like you boys to pick those mangoes before they get too ripe. Your mother wants to make mango bread, Alani. Why don't you and Brian — "

They heard Auntie Mary cry out. Then, a mo-

58

ment later she rushed back to the table. She looked frightened.

"That was Evelyn Fernandez. She says she just found Alfredo lying in their garden, unconscious. She thinks he's had a heart attack!"

7

Everyone ran out the door after Auntie Mary. The Fernandez house was just a few hundred yards away, across the road.

Auntie Mary ran up the front steps and pounded on the front door. "Evelyn?"

Evelyn Fernandez came to the door. "It's all right now," she said in a shaky voice. "Alfredo came to while I was on the phone."

"Where is he?" Uncle Joe asked.

"In the bedroom. I helped him into the house and made him lie down."

"He shouldn't have been moved," Auntie Mary said sternly. "I'll take a look at him."

She disappeared into the house. Uncle Joe looked at the children. "Kupuna and I will go back home," he said. "You boys stay here in case you're needed. You come with us, Maile."

Maile started to protest until she saw the expression on her father's face. "Those chickens need to be fed, young lady."

Brian, Keone, and Alani sat on the front porch, waiting to be told what to do next. In a few minutes, Auntie Mary called them into the house.

"Uncle Alfredo is very weak," she said. "But he's better than I expected. He wants to ask you boys a question."

The boys filed silently into the bedroom. Uncle Alfredo was sitting up, surrounded by pillows. As weak as he was, he seemed tense and nervous. When he saw the boys, he motioned for them to come closer. "Did any of you hear something strange last night?"

"Wh-what do you mean, Uncle?" Alani asked, glancing at Brian.

Alfredo struggled to sit on the edge of the bed. His wife tried to push him gently back on the pillows, but he shook her off.

"Alfredo!" Auntie Mary said.

"Be quiet, Mary!" he said crossly. "Well, boys?"

"Uh . . . Brian. . . . " Alani swallowed hard and nudged his friend.

Mr. Fernandez stared at Brian. "Well, boy? Did you see or hear something strange?"

Brian nodded slowly. "I-I thought I did, but — "

"But what?"

"But maybe it was just a bad dream," Brian said.

Alfredo made a sound of disgust. "It was no dream! I know what I heard. And what I saw. The night marchers again."

Alani gasped.

"That's enough," Auntie Mary said. "What are you trying to do, Alfredo? Scare us all?"

Alfredo nodded. "You should be scared, Mary. We should all be scared. Kupuna says I'm crazy, an old fool. But I know what I know. This valley is cursed!

"Last night, I woke up hearing drums and chanting. At first I thought I'd only imagined it. But the noise went on and it came closer and closer. I got up and looked out the window. And I saw — I saw — " His face turned gray and his hands began to tremble.

"Stop it!" Evelyn cried out. She was close to tears.

"No, no, I must tell you what I saw. They were walking along the road, single file, and they were dressed the way the ancient Hawaiians dressed.

But . . . " He paused, and his voice dropped to a low whisper. "Their bodies were glowing!"

They stared at him, speechless.

"You don't believe me?" he cried, looking from one to another. "Go on, then. Look out the window. Look at the garden."

They moved to the window and stared at the plants. The leaves and stems were brown and withered, as if a plague had struck.

"I didn't see that until this morning," Alfredo went on in a more normal voice. "Last night, when I saw the procession, I was terrified. I crept back to my bed and hid. This morning when I woke up I almost thought it was a dream, until I went outdoors and saw the garden." He rubbed a shaky hand over his face. "I must have fainted. The next thing I knew, my wife was bending over me."

He collapsed back against the pillows. Evelyn burst into tears. "He-he's right," she sobbed. "It must be the curse of the ancient Hawaiians. Yesterday that garden was so healthy. We had the best tomato crop we've had in years. Now — "

Auntie Mary put an arm around Evelyn and led her from the room. The boys followed.

In the parlor, Auntie Mary helped Evelyn into

a chair. "We must get Alfredo to a doctor. Keone, you boys go clear out the back of his pickup truck. You know what a mess it is. He'll need to lie down, so we'll put some cushions and blankets in back." She sounded like a general giving orders. But no one argued.

When the boys reached the battered old truck, Brian saw what Auntie Mary had meant by a mess. He wrinkled his nose. The truck even smelled bad. And it was filled with fishing nets, tools, cans, and bottles of garden chemicals, like bug sprays and weed killer. There were a couple of plastic pails and a thermos jug. Brian started to open the thermos, but Keone warned him not to. "You don't know how long it's been lying in the truck, in the hot sun. Whatever's inside probably turned to mold a long time ago."

"Yuck," Brian said, dropping it.

When the boys had emptied the back of the truck, Keone went to find blankets and pillows. The boys made a comfortable bed for Alfredo. Auntie Mary and Evelyn helped the sick man out to the truck. Although Alfredo kept protesting that he was fine and didn't need to see a doctor, Brian saw that he leaned heavily on the two women for support.

Auntie Mary directed Keone to ride in back with Alfredo. She and Evelyn climbed in the front, Auntie Mary at the wheel. "Alani, you and Brian go home and tell your father and Kupuna where we're going."

Brian and Alani watched the truck disappear down the rutted road before they trudged back to their own house. On the way, Alani said, "I guess I owe you an apology."

"What for?"

"For kidding you about having a dream. You really did see the night marchers."

"I didn't see them, but I heard them," Brian said.

"No wonder you were scared. Man, I would have been petrified! I guess Alfredo is lucky. Remember what Kupuna told us about people who see the night marchers?" He shivered. "He could have been killed."

"There must have been someone in the procession to protect him," Brian said. "One of his ancestors."

Alani shook his head. "I don't see how. He's not Hawaiian, he's Portuguese. His parents came here when he was a little boy."

"But — " Brian frowned, puzzled. Before he

could finish what he was going to say, he heard Alani groan.

"Maile! That dumb kid!"

Brian saw that one of the chickens had gotten out of the fenced-in yard. Maile was running after it, trying to shoo it back, but the chicken was not cooperating.

"Come on," Brian said, "let's go help her. She'll never catch that chicken by herself. It's almost as big as she is!"

Alani laughed and the boys broke into a run.

After they captured the chicken, Brian remembered that they had a message from Auntie Mary for Uncle Joe and Kupuna. He went to the garden to find them.

The two men were carefully weeding a patch of new lettuce plants. As soon as they saw Brian, they stopped, resting on their hoes. When Brian related the strange story Alfredo had told, Kupuna looked badly shaken. Uncle Joe just shook his head. "The whole thing sounds crazy to me," he said. "I'm going over there to take a look at that garden."

Brian turned to Kupuna. "I don't understand why Uncle Alfredo didn't die. Remember what you told us about — "

"None of this makes any sense," Kupuna exclaimed. He put his hand on Brian's shoulder. Brian wasn't sure if it was meant to comfort him or if it was the grandfather who needed reassurance. "The night marchers are spirits, Brian. They don't curse the living and they don't ruin crops. None of this makes any sense."

"Maybe Uncle Alfredo just dreamed it," Brian said, trying to find something to say to reassure both of them.

"Those tomato plants were no dream," Kupuna said. "And remember what you told us you heard? Was that a dream?"

"I-I don't know," Brian said. He felt miserable. Kupuna had looked so tall and proud when Brian first arrived. Now he seemed old and ill and Brian was worried.

"Nor do I," Kupuna said softly. "I don't understand any of this."

"I have to help Alani," Brian said.

Kupuna nodded but Brian wasn't sure the old man had really heard him.

The rest of the morning passed quietly. It was early afternoon when they heard a truck stop in front of the house. It was Uncle Alfredo and Auntie Evelyn. Alfredo looked much better. The color was back in his face, and his hands did not shake.

"I'm sound as a bell," Alfredo said with a broad smile, thumping his chest. "The doctor can't understand it. Oh, well, what does he know?"

"More than an old farmer," Evelyn snapped. Unlike Alfredo, Evelyn did not look happy. "The doctor wanted Alfredo to go into the hospital in Honolulu for a complete checkup."

Kupuna frowned. "Alfredo, is this true? Did the doctor — "

"Bah! He knows nothing. Listens to my heart and says I'm strong as a horse. Takes my pulse and says nothing wrong there. Blood pressure, perfect! So, when he can't find something wrong, he wants to send me to another quack."

"Maybe you should do as he says," Kupuna said. "You aren't a young man, my friend."

"Oh! And who would take care of the garden while I'm gone? Those tomato plants will have to be pulled out and new ones put in! And what about the goat? Do we ignore him while I lie around in a hospital? And the pigs? And the — "

"We'll help, Kupuna," Keone said eagerly. "We can take care of things for you, Uncle Alfredo."

It was a generous offer, but Brian could see

that Alfredo was not very pleased. "It won't be necessary," Alfredo said abruptly. He seemed upset by the offer. "No, I've made a decision that makes me feel like a new man!"

"What decision?" Kupuna asked.

"I'm going to sell my farm and move out of the valley. I'm getting too old for this way of life. Time to retire."

"What?" Kupuna leaned forward as if he could not believe what he had heard.

"Last night was a warning," Alfredo said. "The valley no longer wants us, Kupuna! Times have changed and we must change, too. This way of life is dying for us. Time to move on!"

Kupuna looked stunned.

"Sell?" Kupuna whispered. "Alfredo, you can't be serious."

"But I am." Alfredo stood up and stretched. "Well, time we went home. There's work to be done. But not for long. Soon we'll be able to get up when we want to and go to bed when we like. We'll be able to spend our money on something other than seedlings or fertilizer. And there'll be no goat to scold me if his breakfast isn't ready on time! Ah, that will be the day!"

When the visitors had driven away, Keone

tapped Kupuna on the shoulder. "Do you think Uncle Alfredo really means what he said?" Keone asked uneasily.

"I don't know," Kupuna said. "He's not the first one to talk about leaving the valley."

Maile crawled into Kupuna's lap. "Does that mean we won't ever see them again?" she asked.

"Oh, Maile, don't ask such dumb questions," Alani snapped.

"It's not a dumb question," Kupuna said softly, hugging Maile to him. "The land in this valley is precious. It is more than just dirt and weeds and rocks. It is a way of life! But if the families leave the valley, others will move in and who will they be? What will they do? What we have now will be lost forever!"

8

A week later, it seemed like everything was back to normal. But Brian could sense that under the surface things had changed.

One evening Uncle Joe and Kupuna went to a meeting of the farmers. When they came home, they were both very upset. Not only had Uncle Alfredo decided to sell his land, but he had convinced several more families to do the same. About half the families in the valley were getting ready to leave.

Uncle Joe was angry. "What's the matter with them?" he said. "How can they give up so easily?"

"They're afraid," Auntie Mary said. "Nothing like this has ever happened before. They feel helpless."

"But where will they go?" Uncle Joe said. "Into

the city? To live on crowded streets? To send their children to crowded schools?"

"I don't suppose all of them will move to the city," Auntie Mary said. "Some of the neighbors are talking about moving to Kalawa. It's not a bad little town, Joe."

Uncle Joe and Kupuna stared at her in surprise.

"Times change," Auntie Mary said. "Farming isn't the only way to make a living."

"And what does that mean?" asked Uncle Joe.

"Only that moving to Kalawa might not be so bad. If we lived in town, we'd be closer to the schools and the beach. I wouldn't have to drive so far to work."

"And what would I do?" Uncle Joe said angrily. "Sit all day in the shade and twiddle my fingers?"

"There are plenty of jobs in Kalawa. You're good with your hands, Joe. You like working with machinery as much as plants. You're good at building things. You — "

Kupuna looked furious. "Are you suggesting that we sell our farm, too?"

"No," Auntie Mary said. "I'm just saying that farming isn't the only way of life." She got up and walked out of the room. Uncle Joe went after her, but Kupuna slumped back in his chair.

Brian felt terrible about what was happening in the valley. In the short time he'd been here, he'd begun to feel like part of the family. He didn't want to see the Nakoas' way of life destroyed, but he didn't know what he could do to help. No one knew what to do.

That night Brian woke up suddenly. At first, he couldn't imagine what had disturbed him. In fact, he was rather annoyed. He'd been having a good dream and wanted to get back to it. He closed his eyes, trying to relax, hoping he'd fall asleep and step right back into the dream. Outside he heard the crickets. They made a comforting, lulling sound and Brian began to drift to sleep.

And then Brian heard something that made him sit up in bed. Drums, a slow, dull thudding in the distance. Chanting of voices, low and monotonous. Drums and chanting, coming closer!

Brian slid out of bed and knelt beside Alani's cot. He shook his friend roughly. "Wake up, Alani!"

"G'way," Alani murmured sleepily. He didn't even open his eyes.

"Alani!" His friend finally blinked and frowned.

"What's the matter?" he muttered.

"Listen."

For a moment Alani just blinked. Then he gasped when he heard the ghostly marchers. "Is that — "

"Yeah," Brian whispered. "Look!" He pointed toward the screen. Out of the darkness, coming from the old trail and moving toward the Nakoa farm, was a ghostly line of figures. Figures that glowed with an eerie, whitish-green light!

9

"Quick! Hide!" Alani didn't wait to see if Brian would hear his warning. He dived under the covers, making a small, shivering lump in the middle of the bed.

Brian crawled back into his own bed, pulled the covers over his head, and lay as still as possible, listening to the dull, insistent thudding of the drums.

Then, little by little, the sounds began to fade. When the night was silent again, Brian pushed the covers away. He sat up very cautiously. It felt good to breathe in the cool, sweet air instead of the hot stuffy air under the covers. Alani heard Brian moving, and he, too, sat up and took a deep breath.

"Are they gone?" Alani whispered.

"It seems like it," Brian whispered back. For

a moment both boys waited, listening, tensed to dive under the covers again. But all they heard were the crickets. Alani scrambled out of bed. "Come on," he said.

"Where are you going?"

"To see if my family is okay."

Brian went with Alani. They woke Auntie Mary and Uncle Joe, then Kupuna, then Keone and Maile. Everyone was fine, although Keone was annoyed at being woken up in the middle of the night.

Uncle Joe went to the *lanai* and peered out into the darkness. "I don't see anything," he said.

"They were there, Dad. Walking right by our house. They looked just the way Uncle Alfredo said. They were dressed like the ancient Hawaiians and — and — " he gulped " — they looked awful. Like rotting corpses." He shuddered and so did Brian. It was a good description.

Uncle Joe looked at his son and one eyebrow went up. "Are you sure you haven't been watching too many horror movies, Alani? Or maybe you ate too much for dinner and had a bad dream as a result?"

"Dad, we both saw them! Brian and I couldn't have had the same dream at the same time."

"Hmmm." Uncle Joe looked out through the screen again. Then he shrugged. "Well, I don't know what to say, son. I didn't hear a thing. Neither did your mother. She would have woken me up if she had."

"Kupuna, didn't you hear anything? Maile? Keone?" Alani looked from one to the other. They all shook their heads.

"You do believe us, don't you?" Brian asked.

No one said anything. Uncle Joe sounded tired. "Let's all go back to bed. It will be dawn soon and time to get up. I'd like to get some more sleep."

"Kupuna, you believe us, don't you?" Alani said.

The grandfather sighed. "I don't know what to think, Alani. I was sound asleep till you woke me up. But don't forget, my bedroom is on the other side of the house. So are the others. You boys are closer. Still — "

Brian and Alani waited tensely. Kupuna shook his head slowly. He looked bewildered. "I was sure Alfredo and the others were just talking nonsense," he muttered. "Now, I don't know. I just don't know."

"We aren't going to settle this by standing

here," Uncle Joe said. He yawned. "We'll talk about it in the morning."

The others shuffled back to their rooms. Maile was the last to go. Just before she left, she turned to Brian. "I believe you," she said. He saw how afraid she was, and suddenly he began to have doubts. Had Alani and he somehow imagined the whole thing? Had they frightened Maile for no reason?

For a long time after everyone went back to bed, Brian lay awake, staring at the dark ceiling. None of this seemed real. It was like a terrible dream. What was going on in Wailele Valley? Why was it being threatened? He was, again, overcome by that feeling of helplessness!

Brian overslept. When he woke up, the sun was already riding high over the horizon. The family was up, but for the first time since Brian had arrived, they were quiet and subdued.

"What's wrong, Auntie Mary?" Brian saw that her eyes were red, and he knew she'd been crying.

"The garden — " Uncle Joe choked on the rest of his words.

Brian stared at the adults waiting for Uncle Joe to finish.

"Half the garden is destroyed," Auntie Mary said bitterly.

"Beautiful plants, all brown today, all dead, just as if they had been killed by a plague."

Maile began to whimper. She ran to her mother and buried her face against Auntie Mary's arm. Mrs. Nakoa put her other arm around the little girl to comfort her.

"Kupuna," Alani said, "you told us the night marchers don't do things like that."

"I know what my grandfather told me about the *Huaka'i po*," he whispered hoarsely. "Among all the stories I heard, none were like this."

Auntie Mary sank into a chair, pulling Maile into her lap. "Well, I think it's time we talked about our future here in the valley. We've lost a lot in one night! Joe, we were counting on those crops to bring us the money we needed. My salary won't cover our expenses. How can we go on?"

Uncle Joe shook his head. "I don't know, Mary."

"Maybe Alfredo is right," Auntie Mary went on. "We have to consider it, Joe. We have to think about —" She choked on her words but she made herself go on. " — about leaving the valley."

Brian could hardly believe what he was hearing. Worse, Uncle Joe didn't try to argue with his wife. Instead, he nodded. "Maybe you're right," he said.

Brian looked at Kupuna to see how he would react. But the old man seemed to be shriveling up inside, like the ruined plants in the garden.

Brian went to the *lanai* to look out through the screen door. From where he was standing he could only see the edge of the garden. He wanted to see it all.

He opened the door quietly, tiptoed down the steps, and walked slowly toward the garden. At first glance everything seemed normal. The chickens scratched and cackled. Hupo lay with his head on his paws, his tail flicking at small flies. A breeze played over the grass and bushes.

Auntie Mary's description had not really prepared Brian for the horror of the garden. Yesterday's bright, new, green lettuces were now brown and limp. Stalks of green onions were lying in their rows like fallen soldiers. The green foliage of healthy tomato plants was now curled and withered. Brian swallowed hard. He felt as if he were about to cry.

It made no sense! How often had he heard Kupuna say those words? It made no sense. The night marchers marched to places they had known in life. To fishing places, to sacred places. They marched to greet a new spirit to their ranks; they marched to the sites of old battles. They followed the old trails as they had in life, with a destination and a purpose that did not include destroying a way of life for their descendants.

Then, out of the corner of his eye, Brian saw something that made him want a closer look. He moved right up to the fence and looked through the wire. There, in the soft, well-turned soil, was something that surprised him. A human footprint. A footprint of a bare foot. And it was large enough to have been made by a man.

That was strange, Brian thought. All the Nakoas wore shoes when they worked in the garden. Keone wore tennis shoes, Uncle Joe wore boots, and Kupuna wore rubber thongs that he called slippers.

Brian also knew that in Hawaii, people always remove their outdoor shoes before entering a house. This was a custom that had been introduced by the Japanese when they first immigrated to Hawaii. It was a custom that made good sense, too. It kept the floors and rugs of the household much cleaner.

No one in the Nakoa household — nor anyone in the valley — would go barefoot in the garden. So why was this large footprint of a bare foot imbedded in the earth?

Curious now, Brian went into the garden. But as he did, he noticed that the gate was already standing open. The gate was always kept shut! No one wanted Hupo or any of the chickens to get into the garden by accident. The plants were too precious.

Brian stared at the open gate. Maybe one of the adults had left it open this morning. Maybe in their shock at seeing the ruined plants, they had forgotten to close it. This was possible, but Brian doubted it.

He walked carefully between the rows of vegetables. He found more footprints and tried to imagine ghostly figures moving up and down the rows of plants, passing a hand over the healthy vegetables and blighting them as if by magic. Then he shook his head.

The night marchers would not have destroyed the plants. Nor would they have needed to open a gate nor would they have left footprints! They were ghosts, spirits, and Kupuna had said they always seemed to walk above the ground.

But these footprints were all too real. Some human had left them here. Brian felt a surge of anger. Someone — not something — was trying to destroy this valley.

10

Brian stood in the garden, trying to figure out what to do next. There was something mysterious going on, and he wished he could get to the bottom of it. He was convinced that the answers lay deep in the valley. That's where he had to go.

But he'd promised not to go on the trail. He didn't think he could convince Uncle Joe to take him into the valley. And Kupuna was in no shape to go. Keone? Brian rolled his eyes, knowing what Keone would have to say! Alani, then. No, that wasn't the answer. He knew Alani would get in too much trouble if he disobeyed his family. And right now, Brian didn't want to make things any harder for his friend.

Brian sighed. He knew that if he wanted to find the answers, he'd have to do it on his own, even if it meant breaking his promise to Kupuna. It was the only way. And maybe, if he worked fast, he could explore the valley and be back before anyone realized where he'd gone.

Brian entered the house as quietly as he could. For a few moments he stood in the kitchen, listening. The family was gathered in the parlor. They were arguing about whether or not to sell the land.

Brian didn't waste any time. He made some sandwiches and filled a small thermos with water. He added an apple to his collection of supplies. Now he just needed something to carry the food in. He remembered there was a lightweight nylon backpack in Keone's room.

Brian tiptoed into the parlor and moved swiftly toward the hall. Luckily, none of the adults looked at him as he crossed the room. Even Keone and Alani paid no attention. Only Maile, curled up in the chair next to her mother, followed him with her eyes.

Once in the hall, Brian hurried to Keone's bedroom. He found the backpack and rolled it into a little ball that he stuffed under his shirt. He crossed his arms over the lump it made.

When he walked back through the parlor, Maile

watched him with curiosity. Oh, well, she was probably bored with the adults' talk, he thought. And it didn't matter much what Maile thought. She was only a little kid. It was the adults Brian was worried about but they didn't seem to care what he was doing. This was going to be easy!

In the kitchen, Brian stuffed the food and thermos into the backpack. He went out to the *lanai* and pulled on a pair of jeans. They might feel awfully hot but they would protect his legs on the trail. He pulled on heavy socks and his tennis shoes and tied his windbreaker around his waist. He was glad he'd thought to pack it before he left California. He slipped his arms through the straps on the backpack. Then, feeling like an explorer setting out on a great adventure, he left the house.

Brian made good progress on the road that led to the trail. When he reached the point where the road ended and the trail began, he stopped. If he was going to change his mind and turn back, now was the time to do it. The trail looked harmless enough. Of course, it was overgrown and Brian couldn't tell what he would encounter.

At the last moment, he turned to look at the road behind him. Something moved near a clump of banana trees. He frowned, wondering who it could be. But he saw no more movement and decided it was probably just one of the farmers. He hoped he hadn't been spotted. He waited for a minute more to see if anyone would come after him. No one did. Brian moved toward the trail.

Kupuna had not exaggerated when he said the old trail was dangerous. It looked as if no one had cleared it for years. At times it was hard to tell where it went. After a while Brian lost all sense of direction. The trail seemed to zigzag back and forth at the edge of the valley where the more level ground met the rise of steep-sided hills. Before long, Brian's legs were sore and he was very tired.

He stopped to rest on a soft bed of dead leaves in the shade of a large tree. Slowly he eased the backpack from his aching shoulders. Oh, that felt good! He pulled the thermos from the backpack and took a small sip of cool water. As thirsty as he was, he knew he should use it with caution. He had to make it last a long time.

Overhead, birds chattered in the branches. Insects hummed in the flowers of a nearby bush. Brian was beginning to feel drowsy with the heat when suddenly he heard a rustling in the foliage by the trail. He sat up a little straighter, wondering what it was.

He remembered Kupuna and Uncle Joe talking about the *pua'a*, the wild pigs that lived in the upper reaches of the valley. Brian stiffened. Wild pigs could be dangerous. The boars had sharp tusks that could gore a person with a single sweep.

The bushes rustled loudly again. Something was definitely moving through them. Brian didn't know whether to stand up and run or stay right where he was. He glanced up at the branches of the tree. Did he have time to try to climb up into them?

The bushes moved just a couple of feet from where he sat. Brian took a deep breath and slowly stood up. He crouched, ready to grab the lowest branch, when suddenly something red and blue broke through the bushes. It was no *pua'a*. It was Maile!

Brian nearly exploded! "Maile, you little creep! You scared me half to death," he yelled. "What are you doing here?"

"Following you," she said, as she brushed leaves and dust from her red shirt and blue jeans.

"What?"

"I thought you were acting kind of strange when you came into the parlor. Then, when you came back, I saw the strap of Keone's backpack hanging down under your shirt." She giggled. "You aren't a very good sneak, Brian."

He felt his cheeks burn. "But how did you know what I was going to do?"

"I went into the kitchen and saw the mess you'd made. Bread crumbs and peanut butter on the counter. It wasn't hard to figure out you were going somewhere."

Brian felt like a deflated balloon.

"Okay, so you figured it out," he said. "Now you can turn right around and go home."

She shook her head. "Not till you tell me where you're going and why."

"That's none of your business. Go home!"

"Nope!" She sat down cross-legged with her arms folded defiantly across her chest. "Come on, Brian, you have to tell."

Brian sighed. He was beginning to see why Alani and Keone were usually so annoyed with their little sister. She was being a royal pain!

"If I tell, will you go home?"

"Maybe."

"Promise?"

She thought for a moment and then she shrugged. "Okay."

So Brian told her about how he found the gate to the garden standing wide open and the footprints of bare feet inside.

Maile's eyes grew wide. "That sounds like someone was walking around in the garden, Brian. No one in our family ever leaves the gate open. You know the rule."

Brian nodded. "I agree. That's what makes me think that it wasn't the night marchers who destroyed those vegetables. Someone living did it."

"It couldn't be anyone in the valley," Maile said.

"Why not?"

"Because!" She shrugged helplessly. "We're a family, Brian. And besides, everyone's been hurt by what's happened. Why would anyone in the valley want to hurt themselves?"

"I don't know, Maile. Maybe it isn't someone in the valley. Maybe it's someone who lives outside."

"But you said the figures you saw came from this direction. So how could they get into the valley without anyone seeing or hearing them?"

"I don't know." He felt helpless, not being able to answer her questions. "That's why I'm going into the valley. I'm going to follow this trail and see where it leads."

"I know where it leads."

"You do?" Brian stared at her in surprise.

She smiled. "Sure. I've been on the trail with Kupuna. He took me to see the waterfall and the old *heiau.*"

"The what?"

"A *heiau* is a temple. It was built out of stone by our ancestors. It's a sacred place, like a church."

"Okay, that's great," Brian said. "You can tell me how to get to the waterfall."

Maile shook her head slowly. "Uh-uh. I'm coming with you."

"No way," Brian said. "You promised to go home if I told you what I was doing. Now I've told you, so you have to go home."

"Nope!" She stuck her chin out defiantly.

"You promised," Brian shouted.

"Sure, just like you promised Kupuna that you wouldn't explore the old trail by yourself. You aren't keeping your promise, so why should I?"

"Because," Brian spluttered, "it's too dangerous for a little kid." Then he saw the look on her face, and he wished he hadn't said that.

"Look," Maile said, "let's face it, Brian, you need me. I know the way and you don't."

"But —"

"You have to take me along, even if I am a little kid."

Brian groaned. "Okay, I'm sorry I said that." He felt his cheeks burn and he saw the satisfied grin on Maile's face. "Please! Go home. If anything happened to you, your family would never forgive me."

"Don't worry, nothing's going to happen. I told you, I've been on the trail before."

"Oh, all right," Brian said crossly. He adjusted his backpack and scowled. He hated having the responsibility for Maile, but at the same time he did need her. Besides, there was no way he could make her go back unless he went with her. And he had no intention of abandoning his search now.

"How long will it take to get to the waterfall?" he asked.

"A few hours because the trail is so hard to follow."

"Oh, great!" He felt his spirits sink. How long

would it be before someone realized they were missing? And what would happen then? Brian glared at Maile. "You'd better be prepared to keep up with me," he threatened. "I don't want a little kid to slow me down."

Maile just grinned.

11

The trail seemed to go on forever. After a while Brian was struck with the eerie feeling that he was going to spend the rest of his life on this trail, forever pushing branches aside, forever tripping over small stones, forever walking. Like the night marchers!

It seemed like hours had passed, but the position of the sun told Brian that it was not yet noon. The trail climbed more steeply now and the ground was damp and spongy. The plants were lush here. Great clumps of green ferns carpeted the sides of the trail. Vines hung from the trees and Brian was amazed to see wild orchids. The air was cool and damp, and any other time he would have enjoyed the walk. But today the thick growth only served to slow them down, and he was anxious to get to the waterfall.

Suddenly Maile, who was leading the way, stopped. Brian almost bumped into her. "Why are you stopping?" he asked.

"Someone has cleared the trail," she said. "Look, they cut away all the vines and branches."

Sure enough, where there had been a particularly thick clump of growth, someone had chopped and hacked it back.

"I wonder who's been here?" Maile said, and Brian saw that she was uneasy.

"Kupuna said that sometimes people come into the valley to do some mountain climbing," he said.

"There haven't been any strangers here for a long time," Maile said. "We always know when strangers come to the valley."

Brian shrugged. "Well, it couldn't be the night marchers," he said. "They're ghosts."

Maile shivered. "Don't say that."

"Sorry." He'd meant it as a joke, but here, where the growth overhead was thick enough to block the sun's rays, where the silence was broken only by an occasional bird cry or a mysterious rustling near the edge of the trail, it wasn't funny.

"Well, we aren't going to find the answers by standing here."

Maile nodded and moved on, but Brian could see that she was a little nervous.

The trail began to rise steeply. Brian and Maile had to use clumps of ferns and branches as handholds. The trail seemed darker and more ominous than ever. It had rained recently up here and water dripped with a soft *plop-plop*.

Suddenly Maile cried out and Brian saw her slip on a slick patch of mud. Her arms flailed and he immediately put up his own arms to catch her if she fell back. But she grabbed for an outcropping of rock that jutted up by the trail and managed to catch her balance.

"Are you okay?" he asked.

She didn't answer and he saw that she was looking at her hand with a puzzled expression.

"What's wrong?" he asked. "Did you cut yourself?"

"No, but look!" She held out her hand, and Brian saw something white smeared across her palm.

"What is it?" he asked.

"I don't know. Oh, yuck, it's sticky." She rubbed her hand on her pants leg, smearing the white stuff over the denim. "Ugh! It won't come off. What is it?"

Brian took her hand and looked at it more closely. The white stuff had a funny smell, strange and yet somehow oddly familiar.

"How did you get it on your hand?" he asked.

"When I grabbed the rock," she said. "Look, there's more of it."

Brian couldn't remember where he'd smelled that odd smell before. Finally he said, "Oh, I don't know. But it'll come off."

Maile looked doubtful. "How do you know?"

"I just know." He was getting impatient. They were wasting time standing here talking. "Come on, it's getting late."

Brian was beginning to regret his decision to follow this trail to the waterfall. It was taking too long! And what if, when they reached the end of the trail, they found nothing? He'd broken his promise to Kupuna. Worse, he'd allowed Maile to come with him. He had a sinking feeling that if they ever got out of this mess, he was going to be in big trouble.

"Brian, look!" Maile's excited cry interrupted his thoughts. Then he saw what she was pointing at — a large clearing and the waterfall!

The cliffs that ringed the valley rose stark and straight. Over the top fell a huge sheet of clear water. The soft winds blew it into a fine spray and rainbows danced in the falling water. At the base of the cliff, the veil of water plunged into a deep pool that was ringed with plants — beautiful flowers, thick green ferns, and wild fruit trees.

"Oh, wow!" Brian whispered. "It's beautiful here."

"Come on." Maile broke into a run, with Brian following more slowly. He was stiff and sore from the climb. The water looked so inviting. When he saw Maile pulling off her shoes and socks, he did the same.

They sat on a low rock and dangled their hot, tired feet in the cold water. They splashed it over their heads and then splashed each other. It felt wonderful!

"I'm hungry," Maile said.

Brian remembered the lunch he'd packed. It was a good thing he'd brought a lot of sandwiches. "Didn't you bring anything to eat?" he teased, knowing that she hadn't.

"I didn't have time," Maile said. "Besides, I figured you had enough for both of us."

"Oh, yeah? Well, I didn't know you'd be tagging along. So what makes you think there's enough for you?"

Maile put her hands on her hips and cocked her head to one side. "Because I know how you boys eat," she said, in a perfect imitation of Auntie Mary.

Brian laughed. "Okay," he said. He dug into the backpack and brought out the sandwiches. "But just one for each of us," he told her. "We ought to save something in case we get hungry on the way home."

"Okay." Maile nodded as she bit into her sandwich. Then she said, "Have you ever tasted mountain apples?"

"Are you kidding? Hey, in California we have all kinds of apples. Of course I've tasted — "

"Not regular apples," Maile said. "Mountain apples. They look like apples but they taste a little different. Anyway, there's a bunch of them on the trees. Why don't we pick some before we go back?"

Brian groaned. Picking fruit was the last thing he wanted to do. "Go ahead," he said.

He lay back in the soft bed of ferns. Oh, did that feel good!

"Lazy!" Maile said. She picked up the backpack.

"Where are you going with that?" Brian asked.

"I have to put the fruit in something!" She walked over to one of the trees and began to pull the small red fruit from a low branch. Brian watched her for a minute, then he closed his eyes. Boy, was he tired. And sore! He wondered how many miles they'd walked.

"Brian, look!"

Without opening his eyes, he mumbled, "What?"

"More footprints. Lots of them."

His sleepiness vanished. He jumped to his feet and went over to Maile. She was staring at the ground. Sure enough, the damp earth was covered with footprints. But these prints had been made by boots, not bare feet.

"Whoever left these prints must have been the same person who cleared the trail."

"There are too many prints for just one person," Maile said. "It looks like a whole group of people. But how did they get here?"

Brian thought for a moment. "Maybe it was one of the farmers," Brian said. "Someone who came up here to pick the fruit."

Maile shook her head. "I don't think so," she said. "No one comes here very often. Especially not now, not with the night marchers being seen on the trail."

"Why not?"

"Because . . ."

"Because why?"

"Because of the *heiau* and — and the cave." Her voice dropped to a whisper and she looked nervously over her shoulder.

"You didn't say anything about a cave," Brian said excitedly. Caves were great places to explore, as long as you didn't get lost in them. "Where is it?"

"Near the *heiau*," she said.

"And where is the *heiau*?" Brian asked. Why was it so hard to get her to give him an answer?

She pointed to the base of the cliff. "See where the trail goes? It follows the cliff. The *heiau* is on the trail on the other side of those trees."

"Show me." Brian picked up the backpack and thrust his arms through the straps. He wasn't at all tired anymore.

Maile took a couple of steps backward, shaking her head. "No, it's getting late and we have to get home."

"Aw, come on," Brian said. "Just one quick look."

"No!" she said, and Brian heard a note of panic in her voice. "Kupuna says it is a sacred place and we should stay away from it. Besides, that's where — "

"Maile, what are you scared of?"

She took a deep breath and looked again over her shoulder. "That's where the *Huaka'i po* come from, Brian. And see, that's where the footprints go!"

Brian suddenly felt cold. The beautiful, peaceful clearing seemed strangely frightening. As if to underline Maile's words, a cloud slid across the sun, and the bright light in the clearing was dimmed.

"Maybe you're right," Brian said. "It's late and we'd better get back." He hoped he didn't sound as nervous as he felt. By now they had probably been missed. He wondered what Auntie Mary and Uncle Joe were thinking. Would Kupuna suspect where Brian and Maile had gone?

If only they could swim back down the stream, it would be quicker. That gave him an idea. "Why don't we follow the stream back," he said. "It'll take a lot less time than going on the trail."

"I don't know where the stream goes," Maile said.

"It goes downhill, silly. Don't you know that if

you get lost you're supposed to try to find running water and follow it downhill?"

"We aren't lost," Maile said. "And what if we can't get down through the valley that way? You saw how overgrown the trail was."

"Oh, don't be such a scaredy-cat," Brian said. "Come on, I'll go first." He started walking before she could object. He heard her call his name, but he wouldn't stop. Maile was forced to follow or be left behind.

Brian soon discovered that he'd been right. They did save time and the stream wasn't as badly overgrown as they had feared.

"See?" Brian said. "I told you — " He stopped and stared.

"What is that?" Maile asked when she saw what Brian was staring at.

"It's a dam," Brian said. The stream was filled with large rocks and branches of trees. Behind the dam, the water had pooled and spilled over the banks of the stream. Brian saw that it didn't stop all the water from flowing, but it certainly held a lot back.

"What's it doing here?" Maile said.

"More footprints," Brian said excitedly, pointing to the swampy ground. "Maile, someone blocked the stream on purpose. Now it's beginning to make sense!"

"What is?"

"All of it! The footprints, this dam. Don't you see? Someone is deliberately trying to frighten the farmers by ruining their crops and damming up the stream."

"But why?"

"I don't know," Brian said. "But one thing is for sure. Kupuna said the night marchers didn't curse the valley. He said they wouldn't destroy the crops or dry up the stream. He was right! Real people did this, not ghosts."

"We've got to tell my father and Kupuna," Maile said. "They'll know what to do."

"Not yet," Brian said. "There's something else I want to do first, before we go home."

"What's that?"

"Go back to the pool and follow those footprints. I want to know where they end up. Maybe something will tell us who is doing all this and why."

Maile gasped and took a small step backwards. "Oh, no," she said. "No, we can't go back."

"We have to," Brian said. "Don't you see? We need to learn as much as we can."

"Brian, those prints lead toward the *heiau* and the cave."

"So? I'm not afraid of caves."

"B-but this cave is different," she stammered. "It's special. It's a burial cave."

12

Burial cave!

Scenes from horror movies Brian had seen late at night flew into his mind. Scenes of skulls and bones, of skeletons lying in cobwebbed tunnels. Scenes of corpses rising from their graves. Alani's description of the figures they'd seen last night came back to haunt Brian. "Rotting corpses." He recalled all too clearly the procession of figures, glowing with that eerie greenish-white light.

"Burial cave?" he said.

Maile nodded. "That's where our ancestors are buried," she whispered as if afraid of being overheard. But there was no one around to hear her, except Brian. No one living, he thought.

He pushed these scary thoughts away. This

was not the time to let his imagination run away with him.

"That doesn't change anything," he told her. "We still have to go back. Come on."

"Brian, please, no! Look at the sun. It's really getting late. Besides, we're already halfway home. We might as well keep going. We can tell my father and Kupuna and — "

Brian turned and started back the way they had come.

"Brian, come back!" Maile cried.

"You go on home if you want to. I'm going to the cave," Brian said stubbornly.

"But I don't know the way home," she moaned.

"I told you, just follow the stream. You'll be okay."

"Oh, you!" she cried. "Oh, all right. I'll go with you." He heard how angry — and scared — she sounded.

"Look, this won't take long, I promise," he said. "We don't even have to go into the cave. We just have to find where those footprints lead."

Maile didn't answer. She looked very sullen as they began their trek back to the pool.

They didn't stop to rest and they didn't talk.

Each was aware that they didn't have much time. Neither of them wanted to be near the cave when the sun set.

By the time they reached the pool, the sun was already casting long shadows across the ground — long shadows that looked like long, dark fingers. Brian tried to concentrate on following the footprints. He saw that they led past the waterfall and pool, along the base of the cliff. The trail disappeared into a grove of trees, and when they entered the grove, the light dimmed. It was so silent here, so quiet they could hear themselves breathe. Brian couldn't even hear any birds or insects. He told himself it was the presence of humans that had frightened the animals into silence, but deep inside he wasn't so sure.

Suddenly Maile clutched his arm. The feeling of her cold fingers on his skin made him jump. "Don't do that!" he muttered shakily.

"Sorry." She was whispering. "The cave is on the other side of that big rock."

"Let's go," he whispered, hoping he sounded braver than he felt.

They moved cautiously around the big rock. There, in the face of the cliff, was the entrance to the cave. It made Brian think of a large, hungry mouth, opened to take a big bite. He shook himself. If he didn't stop imagining things, he was going to scare himself to death.

They walked slowly toward it. Under their feet the gravel crunched. Other than that, there were no sounds. Brian felt Maile's cold little hand slip into his. He didn't laugh at her or push her away. Instead, his fingers clutched hers.

"You said we didn't have to go inside," she whispered as they reached the entrance.

"Look at the footprints," he said. "They go into the cave."

She moaned and he felt her tremble. "Let's get out of here."

"Not yet." He had to see what was in that cave. "Besides, we already agreed that ghosts don't leave footprints. Only people do."

"What if the people who made the footprints are in there?" she whispered.

Brian hadn't thought about that. Her question made him stop and think. Then he said, "But we haven't heard anyone. I don't think anyone's in there."

Maile whimpered a little but she let him lead

her into the cave. They couldn't go very far, Brian realized, because they didn't have a flashlight. He wished he'd thought to bring one.

There wasn't much to see anyway. Just rough rock walls, damp with moisture. Even the air was damp and chilly. Just like in a tomb, he thought.

"Brian, look!" Maile's startled voice made him jump. He turned to look and saw that she was holding out her hand. The palm glowed with an eerie greenish-white light. Brian noticed that the side of her jeans was also glowing. Then he remembered the white sticky stuff she'd touched on the trail. And suddenly he knew why it had smelled familiar.

"Paint!" he said.

"Paint?" Maile echoed. "What kind of paint glows like that?"

"Phosphorescent paint," he said. "Mom and I used some once to decorate a crazy T-shirt for Dad for his birthday. The paint glowed in the dark."

"But what would phos — " She tried to say the big word and gave up. "What would that stuff be doing on the trail?"

"I don't — " He stopped, suddenly remembering the line of figures that had glowed with an eerie light. At that moment a few more pieces of the puzzle fell into place. "Let's look around," he said. "I think maybe the answer is in here."

Then he spotted several large wooden crates lined up in a row against the rock wall. He hurried to the first one and found that it opened easily. Inside were pieces of material that all smelled of that paint.

"*Malo* and *kikepa*," Maile gasped.

"What?"

Maile explained that the *malo* was a loin cloth worn by the ancient Hawaiian men. The *kikepa* had been worn by the women. "It was like a-a-" Maile fumbled for the right word.

"A *sarong*?" Brian asked, remembering a picture that had been in his fifth grade social studies book.

"That's right. Why are they covered with paint?"

"Maile, it all makes sense," Brian said. "The night marchers Alani and I saw were real people, dressed up to look like ghosts. And I bet they are the ones who wrecked the plants and dammed up the stream. Someone is trying to scare the farmers away for sure."

Inside the other crates they found drums and

nose flutes. There were torches, too. The last crate they opened contained cloaks and helmets and wicked-looking spears. Everything had been crudely painted with the phosphorescent paint.

"Who would wear these?" Brian said, pointing to one of the capes.

"Warriors, going into battle," Maile said. "Kupuna said that sometimes the *Huaka'i po* march to the site of an ancient battlefield." Her voice was filled with awe as she repeated her grandfather's words. "The dead chief may be carried in a *manele*, a kind of string hammock, just the way he was carried in life. Or he may march between two warriors.

"The procession is lighted by torches. Even if it rains, the torches burn brightly because they are ghost torches. At the head of the procession is the spearsman. He calls out a warning to the living to get out of the way. It's his duty to kill any living person who gets caught in their path."

Brian sensed that Maile was repeating the story almost word for word as Kupuna had told it to her. She'd probably heard it so many times she'd almost memorized it.

Still, he felt a chill pass through him as he listened to her words. At home with Kupuna and

Alani and Hupo, the ghost stories had been deliciously scary. But here, in this dark, forbidding cave, it was different.

Brian gulped. Suddenly he wanted to be back outside, out in the bright sunlight and warm air. He stuffed the garments they were holding back into the crate. His hand touched something sharp. He reached into the crate and pulled out a spear. It was crudely made but the point looked very dangerous. Quickly Brian dropped the weapon back into the crate.

"Come on," he said to Maile, "let's get out of here!"

When they stepped out of the cave, they saw that the sun had fallen lower. The trees blocked much of the light, and shadows lay like dark shrouds. There was a slight chill in the air.

Brian took off at a slow run. "Hurry," he called back to Maile. He could hear her footsteps behind him as they entered the grove of trees. Then he heard a scuffling noise and a cry. Maile had slipped on a patch of loose gravel. Brian reached down to help her to her feet but she drew back.

"My ankle!" she groaned.

Brian knelt beside her and tried to remember his first-aid, but all he could think of was to ask her to wiggle her toes. She was able to wiggle them. Brian touched her ankle as gently as possible. "Does it hurt here? What about here?"

At one point she cried out again. "I don't think it's broken. Looks like you only twisted it," he said.

"But it really hurts," she moaned.

"I know." Brian was in despair. Even if it was only a sprain, Maile wouldn't be able to walk by herself. She was far too heavy for him to carry her. And he certainly couldn't leave her here alone. They were trapped!

13

Brian, what are we going to do?" Maile groaned.

He thought quickly. In a few hours it would be dark. The air would be chilly high up in this valley. And Brian wasn't sure what animals might roam the area at night. He knew he'd feel a lot safer if they were in some sort of shelter.

"We'll have to go back to the cave," he said at last. "We can't stay out here."

Maile whimpered, from fear as well as from pain. "Not there!"

"Don't worry," he said. "It will be okay. And it's a lot safer in there than it is out here. Come on, Maile, lean on me and keep your foot off the ground."

He helped her to stand and they went back to the cave, moving slowly and awkwardly. Maile ended up hopping on her uninjured foot, but Brian could see that it jarred her whole body. She winced and bit her lower lip to keep from crying out.

At last they reached the mouth of the cave. Brian lowered Maile to the sandy floor. He took a piece of cloth from the crate and tore off a strip. He wet the cloth with a little of the water in the thermos and wrapped it around her ankle. He hoped that would keep the ankle from swelling. It was the only thing he could do. Then he saw that she was still shivering. He wrapped the windbreaker around her shoulders and sat down beside her.

The sun was setting. In the west the sky had turned from orange to a pale lavender. Brian wished again that he'd brought a flashlight. Then he thought about building a fire. But he had no matches. He remembered the torches in the last crate and, while the light still held, he hurried to search it. But he came up empty-handed.

"Brian, I'm so cold," Maile said.

"I know," he said. "Me, too." He huddled up next to her. Then he remembered the sandwiches and fruit still left in the backpack. He was hungry and he was sure Maile was, too. If they divided the food carefully, there would be enough for tonight with some left over for morning.

They ate slowly. Brian made Maile chew each bite ten times. "If you eat real slow," he told her, "it makes it seem like you're eating more."

And it gave them something to do! Keeping busy took their minds off their troubles, but at last the meal was done. They talked for a while, their voices lowered. The sky grew darker and stars appeared.

"How's your ankle?" Brian asked.

"Better. It doesn't hurt as much," Maile said.

"Why are we talking so softly?" Brian said, forcing a laugh. "No one can hear us." He wanted to make Maile laugh, too, but she didn't say anything. Brian remembered the ancient bones moldering somewhere in the black depths behind them.

"Brian, what if those people come to the cave tonight?"

The phony night marchers! He'd almost forgotten about them. This cave seemed to be a base for their operation, but Brian didn't think they would be back tonight.

"The first time I heard them was the night Uncle Alfredo saw them. That was over a week ago. They didn't come again till last night."

It was hard to believe that he had seen them less than twenty-four hours ago. So much had happened since! Brian thought about his warm, snug bed on the *lanai*. He would have given anything to be in it right now!

"I guess you're right," Maile said thoughtfully. "They don't come every night. I guess we'll be safe here."

Safe enough except for the dead buried at the back of the cave, Brian thought. Then he forced himself to think of something pleasant. He remembered the day he had gone to the beach with Alani, Keone, and Maile — the hot sand, bright sunlight, and all the noise Alani and he had made, laughing and splashing in the warm water. . . .

He realized that Maile had fallen asleep. Her head lay heavily on his shoulder and he could hear her even breathing.

Suddenly he heard a sound in the still night. At first he thought he'd only imagined it, but then he heard it again, a *thock*, *thock* sound.

Next to him, Maile stirred, moaning a little. "What's that?" she whispered.

"Quiet!" His fingers dug into her arm. The sound was getting louder and then Brian recognized it. It was a helicopter, and it sounded like it was landing in the clearing near the pool.

Maile recognized it, too. "Brian, someone's come to rescue us!"

Of course! By now Uncle Joe and Auntie Mary would have become so worried, they would have called the police or fire department. He got to his feet and stretched his cramped muscles. "Stay here," he said. "I'll go find them."

"Don't leave me here alone," Maile begged. "I want to go with you."

She tried to stand up and he heard her say, "Ouch!"

"Don't be dumb, Maile." He pushed her gently back to the ground. "You shouldn't walk on that ankle. Anyway, you won't be alone for long."

"Brian — " Her voice rose in panic.

"Don't be such a scaredy-cat! I won't be gone long and we won't leave you behind, I promise."

Brian stepped out of the cave. A full moon had risen and hung like a huge silver globe in the night sky. Brian thought it looked so close he could almost reach out and touch it.

"Brian!" Behind him, in the cave, Maile's hoarse whisper cut through the darkness. He was about to tell her off but he suddenly choked back his words. He drew quickly back into the cave.

"What — " Maile started to say, but Brian dropped to his knees beside her and put his hand over her mouth.

"Be quiet!" he whispered fiercely. "Listen!"

Men's voices were coming from the trail.

"I'm sick and tired of your whining," one man snarled. "You'll do as you're told."

"Please, let me go! I've done everything else you wanted. But not this! It's too much."

Maile pushed Brian's hand from her mouth. "That's Uncle Alfredo!" she whispered.

Brian nodded, although he realized she couldn't see his movement in the dark. "And that giant we saw with him in Kalawa — the one Alani called Tako," he whispered back. "I recognized them in the moonlight."

"But what is Uncle Alfredo — "

"Shh. We can't let them see us. We have to hide." He thought quickly. There was only one place left! The back of the cave.

Maile might be terrified of the bones of her ancestors, but she was even more afraid of the men who were coming up the trail. She didn't need to be told twice. She struggled to her feet. At the last minute, Brian remembered the backpack.

Brian and Maile moved toward the back of the cave, feeling their way blindly. Suddenly Brian touched an outcropping of rock. Maybe they would be safe behind it. He helped Maile to the other side and lowered her to the ground. Then he huddled beside her.

They were not a moment too soon. The dim light at the entrance darkened as the figures of men crowded into it.

"You said no one would get hurt," Alfredo said. "You promised."

Tako laughed. It was an ugly sound. "No one will get hurt. But that old man still refuses to leave. We've run out of time, Alfredo. Now we have to do something to make him leave."

"If you'll just give me a little more time," Alfredo begged. "I'm sure I can talk him around. After all, the rest of the family is convinced that the ghosts are to blame for all the bad luck in the valley."

"Talk!" Tako sneered. "That's all you're good for, Alfredo. No, I tell you. It's too late for that!"

Tako's words were drowned out by the arrival of other men. "Hey, Tako, give us a hand. This stuff is heavy."

Tako growled. Brian peered around the out-cropping of rock to see what they were doing, but he was blinded by a bright light. He blinked, trying to adjust his eyes. Then he saw that several of the men held battery-powered lamps.

"Okay, you guys. Get into those costumes," Tako said. "And hurry it up."

The men opened the chests and took out the costumes of the night marchers. Then they smeared a whitish substance onto their faces and arms. Brian was willing to bet it was phosphorescent paint. He leaned forward to get a better look and almost lost his balance. Luckily, Maile pulled him back just in time.

"What are we going to do?" she whispered.

"Shh, don't talk," Brian whispered back.

Alfredo started to protest. Cautiously, Brian peered around the edge of the rock again and saw that Tako was leaning over Alfredo. "The night marchers act was your idea, Alfredo. You only have yourself to blame. You said it would work and it hasn't. Now shut up!"

Alfredo shrank back against the rock wall. He was shaking from head to foot, but Brian didn't feel much sympathy for the man. For some reason, Alfredo was working with Tako against the valley families. Brian wanted to kick himself for not realizing it sooner. When he thought back, he saw that the clues had been there all the time, right under his nose.

Brian remembered the first day he'd gone with Alani to see the stream. Alani had said that Alfredo had told the other farmers he'd gone into the valley to see why the stream was drying up, but had found nothing. The farmers had trusted Alfredo and believed him.

Also, when the boys had cleaned out the back of Alfredo's truck, they'd found bottles of weed killer. No wonder all the crops had died.

As for Alfredo's fainting spell, Brian was ready to believe it had been faked. Alfredo had probably wanted everyone to think that he, too, was a victim of the night marchers.

Only Kupuna hadn't believed any of it! Kupuna had never thought the spirits of the ancient people were cursing the land. And now, from what Tako was saying, these men were preparing to do something terrible to Kupuna, something that would really get him out of the valley.

"Okay, is everyone ready?" Tako's voice alerted Brian.

"You guys know what to do. That old house is as dry as tinder. It'll burn fast!"

14

Brian," Maile whispered, her voice breaking, "we have to get out of here. We have to warn my parents. They're going to burn down our house!"

He nodded and put his mouth to her ear. "But not now! If they catch us, Maile — "

She nodded and he felt her relax a little.

"You promised no one would get hurt," Alfredo was saying.

"Relax," Tako said. "There's another meeting of the farmers scheduled for tonight. The Nakoas won't even be home. No one will get hurt."

Brian saw Tako walking around the group of men, examining their costumes. "Good," he said at last. "Looks like the paint has absorbed enough light. You know what to do."

The men turned off the lamps. In a few moments, when Brian's eyes adjusted, he saw the eerie glow of the costumed men brandishing their spears and torches.

"Please, Tako," Alfredo whimpered. "Please don't do this."

"Shut up," Tako growled.

"What about him?" one of the men asked.

"Tie his hands and gag him," Tako said. "I'm sick of listening to him. I'll take him with me, back to the helicopter. After you burn the house down, you come back here. I'll meet you at the clearing with the helicopter." He glanced around the cave. "After tonight, we won't need this place again."

"What about this stuff?" the man asked, pointing to the empty chests.

"We'll come back for it later," Tako said.

"Wait a minute," another man snarled. "You aren't going to let Alfredo get away, are you? He knows who we are and what we've done."

Tako laughed. "Don't worry about him. He won't dare tell what he knows. He's in this as deep as we are. Aren't you, Alfredo?"

Alfredo sank to his knees, sobbing.

The group of men began to leave the cave in pairs. The last ones to go were Tako and Alfredo.

Tako had torn up a *kikepa* and used the scraps of cloth to bind and gag Alfredo. Now he pushed the farmer ahead of him out of the cave.

The moment they were gone, Maile struggled to her feet. She still was careful not to put her full weight on her sprained ankle.

"What are you doing?" Brian hissed.

"We've got to warn my parents before those men burn down our house."

"Maile, wait!" But she pushed by him, limping as fast as she could to the mouth of the cave. Brian knew she'd never make it back in time, not with that sprained ankle. He hated to leave her here by herself, but he'd make better time on his own.

He had to make her understand that she'd have to wait here alone. It was their only chance to warn the Nakoas.

But Maile was hobbling as quickly as she could to the mouth of the cave. She paused there for only a second. Brian grabbed her arm.

"Maile, you've got to wait here. You'll never make it all the way back with that sprained ankle. And you'll hold me up, too. If I go by myself, maybe I can get to your folks in time."

"No! I'm going with you. There's no way I'll

stay here by myself. Besides, what if those men come back?"

"They won't!"

"That's what we said before!"

Brian sighed impatiently. She was right. It was too dangerous to leave her here. "Well, we can't go back by the trail. It would take too long and besides, we might run into the phony ghosts." He chewed his lower lip, thinking. "We'll have to follow the stream like we did earlier."

"But I don't know the way," she said. "What if it's too hard to get through the brush and trees? We don't know what we'll run into in the dark."

Brian had to admit she was right! There seemed to be only one answer. "Maile, please! I can do it on my own. Your ankle will slow us up."

"No!" she wailed more loudly than before.

"Will you be quiet?"

"Why? There's no one around to hear us. Brian, I'm not staying here. You can't make me."

"Maile!" Brian was furious. She wanted him to do the impossible.

"Come on," she said. "We're wasting time."

She hobbled out of the cave with Brian close behind her. He was still trying to think of a way to make her listen to reason when he heard a sudden noise behind them. It was Tako!

The children glanced over their shoulders in horror. Maile screamed and tried to run. Brian grabbed her hand and pulled her along faster.

But it was too late. Tako seized them by the shoulders. "Well, well," he snarled. "What do we have here?"

"Let me go," Maile shrieked.

"Shut up, you little brat. Who are you kids and what are you doing up here at this time of night?"

"Nothing," Brian said quickly. "We-we were hiking and we got lost."

Tako glared at Brian. "I thought I heard voices. Good thing I came back to investigate."

"Please," Maile begged. "Let us go."

"Not right now. I don't want anyone out on the trail. You can wait with me in my helicopter. I'll let you go when I'm good and ready."

He started to drag them in the other direction, but Maile lashed out, grabbed his arm, and bit it. He yelled out in pain and let go of Brian for a split second so he could grab Maile with both hands. In that instant she screamed, "Run, Brian!"

Brian had no choice. As much as he hated to leave Maile, he knew one of them had to get away. He tore away from Tako and ran down the trail.

He glanced over his shoulder. Tako had lifted Maile up and was carrying her under one arm as he ran after Brian. But Maile wasn't making it easy. She clawed and kicked him, trying to free herself. Brian saw that Tako could barely keep his balance.

Brian sprinted ahead, putting everything he had into his own escape. Thank goodness for track practice! He had never thought it would come in handy, but now his body responded the way it did at a meet. Only this time the stakes were much higher!

When he rounded a turn in the trail, he abruptly skidded to a halt. In front of him, looming up out of the moonlight, was a sight he would never forget. It was the *heiau*, the sacred temple of Maile's ancestors!

The huge wall was made of stark black stone. Silver moonlight gleamed coldly from the stones at the top. In some places the wall was twenty feet high; in other places, rocks had become dislodged over the centuries and now lay in heaps on the ground. The shadow that the wall cast was like a black velvet cloak. The ruined structure had an air of power, a power that was stern and forbidding. Brian sensed that the power of the *heiau* was stronger than the power of the man on the trail behind him.

Brian turned quickly to see how close Tako was. To his horror, he saw him barrel around the curve in the trail. He was less than twenty feet away! At that moment Tako saw the wall and the boy. Maile dangled limply from under his arm, all the fight taken out of her. Brian could hear her sobbing. Tako dropped her to the edge of the trail as if she were no more than a bundle of rags. He turned his full attention on Brian.

Brian glanced quickly back at the wall. It was not only tall, it was long and there seemed to be no end to it. Clumps of trees and bushes grew up from the base of the wall as far as Brian could see. The end of the wall was lost in a mass of shadows and plant growth.

There was no place to go but up the wall itself. Brian took a deep breath and ran forward. In the darkness he found handholds and toeholds. In moments he was scaling the wall, but he wasn't fast enough.

Tako lunged toward the wall and seized Brian's foot. Brian almost lost his balance. He scrambled desperately with his hands and one foot to keep a hold of the rock wall but it was no use. Tako yanked him hard and the boy fell. He hit the ground with a thud.

When Brian raised his head, he saw that Maile had managed to get to her feet. She stood by the trail and swayed slightly. She didn't stand a chance if she waited. She had to get away! "Run, Maile," Brian cried, but his voice was weak, no more than a croak.

Tako snarled and turned back to Maile. "Run," Brian whispered. He had no strength left to help her. She scuttled backward. Suddenly she froze. Brian was in despair. Why had she stopped?

Then he saw her drop to the side of the trail and roll onto her stomach. She covered her head with her arms. Tako reached Maile in three strides. He towered over her and reached down to pull her up.

His hand froze in midair. He cocked his head to one side, as if listening. Brian heard the sound. It puzzled him. Why were Tako's men returning so soon? And then his blood turned to ice when he realized what he was really hearing.

The sounds rose and swelled in the silence. An ominous drumming, the high-pitched wail of a nose flute, voices chanting.

Tako straightened up and looked down the trail. Brian saw him stagger back, his hands raised as if to ward off danger.

When Brian saw what Tako had seen, his heart almost stopped.

From nowhere they appeared, a procession of figures marching five abreast. Their dark war cloaks swirled about them, the curve of their woven helmets crowned their ghostly heads. The torches they carried burned blood red in the darkness. Their spears, held high, gleamed in the silver light.

Brian glimpsed shadowy faces beneath the helmets — strong faces, the features carved from stone. Eyes that flashed, lips that curled in fury. With mounting horror, Brian suddenly realized that they marched in perfect rhythm, above the ground! And through their bodies he could clearly see the outlines of trees and rocks. *Ka Huaka'i a ka Po!* The Marchers of the Night!

15

Brian moaned and shut his eyes, covering his head with his arms. A wild wind rose; dust and leaves swirled around him.

He heard the cry, ghostly as the wind. *"O'io!"* Flee the spear! The warning cry of the lead spearsman.

A high-pitched scream echoed in the night. And then there was nothing. Only dark silence.

Brian did not know low long he lay there. Slowly he raised his head. He saw the motionless figure of a man lying on the trail — Tako. Maile was on her feet, staring in horror at the wall behind Brian.

Brian glanced over his shoulder. There was nothing, no one. The night marchers had vanished into thin air.

He pulled himself up to his hands and knees.

He felt weak and dizzy. He reached for the stones and slowly climbed to his feet. For a moment he clung to the wall, trying to regain his strength and balance. His head pounded and his body was bruised and scratched, but otherwise he seemed to be all right. Finally he let go of the wall and found he could stand on his own. Limping a little, he walked slowly toward Maile.

"Maile, are you all right?"

She nodded, her eyes still wide, still staring at the wall. "Did you see them?" she whispered.

He nodded. "Where did they go?"

She pointed toward the wall. "There. Into the *heiau*. Brian, they walked right through the wall!"

He turned slowly and stared in horror at the *heiau*. The wall rose, silent and forbidding, like a sentinel of stone.

Suddenly they heard a dog barking.

"Hupo!" Maile cried and at that moment, the dog bounded out of the shadows. Hupo leaped toward them, like a furry rocket, knocking them over. He straddled first one, then the other, licking their faces with his warm, wet tongue.

Moments later the trail was crowded with men — Uncle Joe, several of their neighbors, as well as a number of policemen. Brian had never felt so happy to see anyone in his life.

Hours later, back in the cozy warmth of the Nakoa kitchen, Brian and Maile could almost believe the whole adventure had been a terrible nightmare. The burial cave and the *heiau* seemed a million miles away.

For once Brian didn't mind being fussed over. Auntie Mary prescribed hot baths and soothing ointment. She examined Maile's ankle and Brian's head and decided neither was badly injured. She fixed bowls of hot, rich soup and all but spoon-fed them. When Maile started to nod off in the middle of her second bowl, Auntie Mary carried her to bed.

"You're next," she told Brian.

Brian tried to hold back a big yawn. As exhausted as he felt, he wanted to ask a million questions.

"How did you find us, Uncle Joe?"

"When we discovered that Maile and you were missing, we formed a search party. Every man in the valley was out hunting for you. When we couldn't find you in any of the usual places, we called the police."

"We couldn't believe that Maile and you would go into the valley by yourselves," Kupuna said sternly. "You made a promise to stay away from the old trail."

Brian hung his head, but then he heard Kupuna chuckle softly. When he looked up, he saw that the grandfather's eyes were twinkling. He knew he had been forgiven.

"While we were searching the old trail," Uncle Joe went on, "we came on the group of men dressed up like night marchers. I don't know who was the most surprised."

"They thought you were going to be at a meeting tonight," Brian said. "They planned to burn this house down."

Uncle Joe nodded. "So they said. Of course the meeting had been called off earlier so we could search for you. Once those men were caught, they couldn't talk fast enough or loud enough. They told us the whole story and where we could find Alfredo and Tako. We realized how much danger you were in and we couldn't move fast enough. Thank goodness we got to you in time!"

"What about Uncle Alfredo?" Brian asked. "Why was he trying to get the people to leave the valley?"

Uncle Joe sighed. "It seems Alfredo borrowed some money from Mr. Lee a few years ago. When it came time to repay the debt, Alfredo couldn't do it. So Mr. Lee forced Alfredo to help him get the people out of the valley. He wanted to build a huge resort here. A hotel, golf course, riding stables, tennis courts. You name it! It would have been a huge tourist attraction and made him a very wealthy man."

"None of us wanted to sell our land and leave the valley," Kupuna said. "So Mr. Lee became desperate. Alfredo remembered the stories of the night marchers that we heard as boys. He thought we could be scared out of the valley. And his plan almost worked."

"What will happen to him now?" Brian asked.

"He's agreed to cooperate with the police. Maybe he won't have to go to prison. But Mr. Lee will!"

"And Tako?" Brian asked.

Auntie Mary came back into the room. "What's this? You're still up? I told you — "

"All right," Uncle Joe said, pushing back his chair. "Come on, boys, time for bed."

Keone and Alani went, protesting mightily.

But Brian stayed at the table for a few more minutes. He wanted to talk to Kupuna alone.

"Tako?" Brian prompted.

"The police think he died of heart failure, Brian. They couldn't find a mark on his body."

The cry of the ghostly spearsman echoed in Brian's mind. "It was the night marchers, Kupuna," he said. "Do you believe me?"

Kupuna nodded. "Other people may not want to believe you. They may say that Maile and you were in such a state of shock your imaginations played tricks on you. But *I* believe your story."

"There's one thing I don't understand," Brian said. "Why didn't the night marchers kill us, too?"

For a moment Kupuna was silent. Then he said, "Maile's ancestors march in that procession, Brian. Undoubtedly one of them spoke for her."

"But what about me?"

"As for you," Kupuna said softly, "I believe that the walls of the *heiau* protected you. It is, after all, a sacred place of great power. Or . . ." He paused and smiled, reaching out to cover Brian's hand with his large, gnarled one. "Or perhaps the spirits of our ancestors sensed something special about you."

"Something special?"

"In just a few short weeks, you have truly become a member of our *ohana*, Brian," Kupuna said, squeezing his hand. "You have become Hawaiian in your heart."